Goodbye Hollywood Nobody

lisa samson

Goodbye
Hollywood
Nobody

Book 4

a novel

NAVPRESS

THINK

For a free catalog
of NavPress books & Bible studies call
1-800-366-7788 (USA) or 1-800-839-4769 (Canada).

www.NavPress.com

NAVPRESS and the NAVPRESS logo are registered trademarks of NavPress. Absence of ®
in connection with marks of NavPress or other parties does not indicate an absence of
registration of those marks.

ISBN-10: 1-60006-222-9
ISBN-13: 978-1-60006-222-3

Cover design by The DesignWorks Group, David Uttley, www.thedesignworksgroup.com
Cover photo by Steve Gardner, Pixel Works Studio
Creative Team: Erin Healy, Darla Hightower, Reagen Reed, Arvid Wallen, Kathy Guist

This novel is a work of fiction. Names, characters, places, and incidents are either the product
of the author's imagination or are used fictitiously. Any resemblance to actual events, locales,
organizations, or persons, living or dead, is entirely coincidental and beyond the intent of
either the author or publisher.

Library of Congress Cataloging-in-Publication Data
Samson, Lisa, 1964-
  Goodbye, Hollywood Nobody / Lisa Samson.
    p. cm. -- (Hollywood Nobody ; bk. 4)
  Summary: After years of traveling to movie sets with her grandmother,
seventeen-year-old Scotty Dawn reunites with her father and together
they search for her mother and for answers to their questions about
faith.
  ISBN 978-1-60006-222-3
  [1. Fathers and daughters--Fiction. 2. Mothers and daughters--Fiction.
3. Christian life--Fiction. 4. Blogs--Fiction.] I. Title.
  PZ7.S1697Go 2008
  [E]--dc22

                                   2008020942

**Published in association with the literary agency of Alive Communications, Inc., 7680
Goddard Street, Suite 200, Colorado Springs, CO 80920 (www.alivecommunications
.com).**

Printed in the United States of America

1 2 3 4 5 6 7 8 9 10 / 12 11 10 09 08

Other Young Adult Books by Lisa Samson

Romancing Hollywood Nobody

Finding Hollywood Nobody

Hollywood Nobody

Apples of Gold: A Parable of Purity

Dedication

To Melody Carlson and Robin Jones Gunn,
because you told me I could do it.

Acknowledgments

Special thank yous to all the wonderful readers who have embraced Scotty and her crazy world. God bless you and grant you peace.

Monday, July 11, 6:30 a.m.

I awaken to a tap on my shoulder and open my eye. My right eye. See, these days it could be one of four people: Charley, Dad, Grampie, or Grammie.

"'Morning, dear!"

Grammie.

Oh well, might as well go for broke. I open the other eye.

"Did you sleep well?"

I shake my head and reach for my cat glasses. "Nope. I kept dreaming about Charley in Scotland." We sent her off with her new beau, the amazing Anthony Harris, two days ago. "I imagined a road full of sheep chasing her down."

"That would be silly. They would have to know she hates lamb chops." Grammie sits on my bed. Yes, my bed. In their fabulous house. In my own wonderful room, complete with reproductions of the Barcelona chair and a platform bed of gleaming sanded mahogany. I burrow further into my white down comforter. I sweat like a pig at night, but I don't care. A real bed, a bona fide comforter, and four pillows. Feather pillows deep enough to sink the *Titanic* in.

She pats my shoulder, her bangled wrists emitting the music of wooden jewelry. "Up and at 'em, Scotty. Your dad wants to be on the road by seven thirty."

"I need a shower."

"Hop to it then."

Several minutes later, I revel in the glories of a real shower. Not the crazy little stall we have in the TrailMama, which Dad gassed up last night for our trip to Maine. Our trip to find Babette, my mother. Is she dead or alive? That's what we're going to find out.

It's complicated.

The warm water slides over me from the top of my head on down, and I've found the coolest shampoo. It smells like limeade. I kid you not. It's the greatest stuff ever.

Over breakfast, Grampie sits down with us and goes over the map to make certain Dad knows the best route. My father sits patiently, nodding as words like *turnpike*, *bypass*, and *scenic route* roll like a convoy out of Grampie's mouth.

Poor Grampie. Dad is just the best at navigation and knows everything about getting from point A to point B, but I think Grampie wants to be a part of it. He hinted at us all going in the Beaver Marquis, their Luxury-with-a-capital-L RV, but Dad pretended not to get it.

Later, Dad said to me, "It's got to be just us, Scotty. I love my mother and father, but some things just aren't complete-family affairs."

"I know. I think you're right. And if it's bad . . ."

He nods. "I'd just as soon they not be there while we fall apart."

Right.

So then, I hop up into our RV, affectionately known as the TrailMama, Dad's black pickup already hitched behind. (Charley's kitchen trailer is sitting on a lot in storage at a nearby RV dealership, and good riddance. I'm hoping Charley never needs to use that thing again.) "Want me to drive?"

He laughs.

Yep. I still don't have my license.

Man. But it's been such a great month or so at the beach. So, okay, I don't tan much really, but I do have a nice peachy glow.

I'll take it.

And Grampie grilled a lot, and Grammie helped me sew a couple of vintage-looking skirts, and I've learned the basics of my harp.

I jump into the passenger's seat, buckle in, and look over at my dad. "You really ready for this?" My heart speeds up. This is the final leg of a very long journey, and what's at the end of the path will determine the rest of our lives.

He looks into my eyes. "Are you?"

"I don't know," I whisper. "But we don't really have a choice, do we?"

"I can go alone."

I shake my head. "No, Dad. Whatever we do, whatever happens from here on out, we do it together."

"Deal."

9:00 a.m.

I open up my backpack and pull out some letters I have to answer. Because, you see, I now have a snail-mail address! Is that cool or what?

Angus has been writing me every week since we parted in Asheville.

Dear Scotty,

Well, it's still okay here in Richmond. I got a job on a nearby farm, baling hay and that sort of thing. It's exhausting. And hey, I played the pipes for a wedding last week and three people came up to me asking for my information. One was for a funeral possibly coming soon, which was sad. But the lone piper is a magnificent way to wrap up a tribute to someone's life.

I make a mental note to look up *lone piper* and see what the heck the guy is talking about. But I can picture him playing at a graveside. He'd be so good at it, so respectful, so Scottish looking.

I've decided not to go to St. Andrews for school this year. Mom is having a hard time adjusting to this new way of life, and I've decided to just take a year at community college.

Uh-oh. Man, I hope he doesn't ruin his life trying to replace his father. Not that Mr. Matheson did much before the divorce to make himself irreplaceable, but still. Maybe Angus is trying to make up for his dad. I can't possibly understand, and I know it.

Anyway, how's everything at the beach? Mom said I can come up for a weekend before school starts. That sound good to you? Let me know. I hope you're doing okay, Scotty.

Love, Angus

That's right. "Love, Angus." I'm kidding. I like the guy, but his life is so heavy right now, I'd be an idiot to read too much into a nebulous letter ending like that. But still, it feels nice.

I write him back, tell him we're going on vacation to Maine and will be back in a week or so. Maybe we can get together after that. Call me on my cell if you need me and all that jazz.

Next I tackle a letter from Megan, who works down at an orphanage in Kentucky. I met her on a plane a few months ago, and she's so different, like she really cares about doing something important with her life. She's sent a short note and a picture from a little boy named Owen of a stick figure with a fireman's hat putting out the flames that are licking through the windows of a pointy roofed house. I think I drew that picture myself once.

So I couldn't manage to get down to the orphanage as soon as I'd hoped, but Dad and I are planning for late July, we think. I write and tell her so. She is the coolest.

I address the envelope with multicolored gel pens, adding flowers and curlicues.

Dad looks over. "Enjoying the whole letter-writing gig, are we?"

"Definitely. It's so much more personal than e-mail."

"It's a lost art, that's for sure. I'm glad to see you bringing it back."

I roll my eyes. "Oh, that's me. Always on the cutting edge."

"Well, it's better than blogging."

"That's for sure." I bap him on the arm. "I didn't know you knew about that."

"Scotty! Why wouldn't you? I tracked you for a year based on your Internet activity."

"Oh yeah. That."

My blog. Hollywood Nobody. I took it off-line last month. I am so done with that. For one, I didn't like myself when I was blogging. Setting yourself up as a critic of other people's lives can make a girl pretty smarmy, even if those lives are a wreck. I should feel sorry for them, not revel in their gruesome behavior.

For two, getting hyperfocused on Hollywood made me feel

bad about myself, physically speaking. Despite how much I championed actresses with normal builds, who forsook the surgeon's scalpel and liposuction vacuum, I couldn't help inwardly comparing myself and always coming up short, even though I knew right well how fake it all was.

For three, there are more important things in life to worry about. Like kids in orphanages in Appalachia or people being sold into slavery. I could go on and on. I think Jesus might be talking to me about that sort of thing, and that sort of thing definitely doesn't fit into the Hollywood blog world.

Good riddance to it too.

Violette Dillinger's new website, designed by *moi*, was nominated for an award. So that's really something to be excited about. She came and visited me at Grammie and Grampie's, and yep, she's still got her head on straight.

"I'm glad to be done with that blog, Dad. Thanks for not coming down on me about it."

"I knew you'd get tired of it eventually."

"You didn't check my e-mail, did you?"

"Nope. Couldn't get past the firewall."

I shrug. "Honestly, it's not like I had a lot of secrets anyway."

It's going to be a long trip. Twelve hours to Jackman, Maine. I Google it and settle in to re-research the place. Of course I've been all over it, but there's not much to report. Maybe something new will pop up.

10:30 a.m.

Text message!

Seth!

Seth: Scty! where r u? srry i hvnt txtd in a whle.

Me: No problem. We're in New Jersey. On our way to Maine.

Seth: Nervus?

Me: Yeah. Where are you?

Seth: In a recrdng studio in nyc doing voice ovr 4 the scorsese mvie.

I turn to Dad. "Can we go into New York City and have lunch with Seth if it works for him?"

"Why not? We'll park here in New Jersey and catch a train in. Find out where he is."

Me: No way! We're in New Jersey driving by. Want us to come in for lunch?

Seth: I break at 12 fr the dy.

"Noon. He's done by noon," I say.

"Ask him where he is."

Me: Can we come and take you to lunch? Where are you?

Seth: Thatd b great. im near times square. txt me whn u gt here.

Me: Having fun?

Seth: Yeah. im wearng rpped jeans and a t-shrt.

Me: You did shower at least, didn't you?

Seth: Yes sctty. sheesh.

Me: I'm just saying, Seth. How's your mom?

Seth: Great. feelng lke new. on some hlth food regime now.

Me: Regime? Or regimen?

Seth: U don't chng do u?

Me: Only a little at a time.

Seth: I wnt 2 hear all about me whn u gt there.

Me? What's he talking about? I mean, he doesn't want to talk about anything but himself? I guess Hollywood really is getting to him. Oh. Wait. Maine. ME. The guy needs to learn how to use caps.

Me: Okay. Karissa's not there is she?

Seth: Dnt wrry. shes not here. c ya soon

Me: 'Bye!

Dad pulls off the exit for I-287. "We'll take the train in from Edison."

"Sounds like you know all about this stuff."

"I lived for a year in New York with Grammie and Grampie when I was in high school. We'd take trains all over the place."

"I didn't know that."

He shrugs. "It was okay. Mom hated it. Dad loved it. But the rents were high, so we took up in Maryland for my last two years of school. So how's old Seth?"

"Fine."

"I'm glad things are square between you two."

"Me too. Most definitely."

A couple of months ago, I had been ready to throw in the towel with old Seth.

An hour later

New York City lies before us like a ghost in the distance, only the Empire State Building visible through the haze.

"Can we go up to the top of that?" I ask.

"Let's see how much time we have."

By noon, having traveled on a train and a subway and our feet, we're waiting in Times Square beneath a screen so large you'd have to pay me a million bucks to have my mug magnified like that for all of New York to see.

"Scotty!"

I whip around. Seth runs down the street toward us and gives me a bear hug. "Man, it's so good to see you!" he says.

"You too!"

The guy gives great hugs. He really does.

He lets go and shakes my father's hand. They exchange pleasantries, and I'm so glad I never went into gruesome detail about what a jerk Seth can be sometimes. Good call. Of course, Dad wouldn't trust him to shine my shoes even if he is older and has absolutely no designs on me whatsoever, but that's how dads are supposed to feel. I think.

"Where would you like to eat?" Seth asks.

"Let's stay close." Dad. "We need to get back on the road."

"I really appreciate you guys coming into the city like this."

Dad points down the street. "How about Roxy's? That okay?"

"Sure." Seth nods.

We set out down the street toward the famous deli. The sign reminds me of a marquis, lines of light bulbs highlighting ROXY in red neon. I wonder how much power it takes just to keep this area going? The power companies must love it.

Inside, caricatures of celebrities line the exposed brick walls, and people are eating quite possibly the largest, most overstuffed sandwiches I've ever seen. I didn't think mouths could open that wide, but when you're talking moist, tender corned beef, there's nothing stopping that!

I'm jangling with excitement. I mean, I'm in a cool deli in NYC with my dad and Seth Haas, who's only gotten one stare in here. Is life great or what?

A towering glass case of desserts practically takes my breath away, and even though cookies the size of dinner plates and brownies with enough gooey frosting to ice a cake are displayed, I'm in New York and I'll take the cheesecake, thank you very much.

Cheese. Cake.

I am just sayin'.

Ten minutes later, because everything goes at light speed in this place, huge corned beef sandwiches on rye sit before Seth and me. Dad got the hot pastrami.

We barely say a word as we start the meal, the fresh-fresh-fresh rye bread sticking to the roofs of our mouths, and man, is this the best thing ever?

Finally. We sit back.

I sigh. "I'm going to have to take my cheesecake to go."

Seth laughs. "Good idea. By the way, I quick called Steve and Edie and told them you all were coming in for lunch, and they say hello. Mom said they'd love to come to the beach this fall. And I'll be in between pictures, so I was wondering if we could all rendezvous there."

"Dad?"

"I don't see why not."

"Great," Seth says.

"I'd better pay the tab." Dad gets up.

"Let me." Seth.

"Nope. I'm still older than you. You'd have to fight me for it, and I think I could take you, son."

We laugh.

Nice, Dad. Nice little fatherly threat there. Let him know who's boss.

Dad heads up to the counter.

"So. Karissa. Have you heard from her?" I ask.

Seth nods. "Yeah."

"Oh, no! Really?"

"Yep."

"What happened?"

"She said she was wrong for treating me like that. She's changed, and she wants to try again."

"And?"

"I don't know, Scotty, I feel sorry for her—"

"Seth!"

"Let me finish, babe."

Babe? *Babe?*

"Sorry." Babe.

"I told her I'd be her friend but that we weren't a good combination. That we seem to bring out the worst in each other."

"What did she say?"

He pulls a napkin out of the holder and begins to shred. "Surprisingly enough, she admitted I was right."

"Is it true she was in rehab again this summer?"

"Yeah. She was fired from her next picture because she consistently showed up late and without her lines memorized in her last film, and word got around. She said maybe it's time for her to get away from Hollywood too."

"Please don't tell me she bought a house at the Delaware beach." I reach for my own napkin and begin to shred.

"No." He laughs. "No. I haven't told her where I live."

"So what did you say?"

"I told her getting away would be just what she needs. So she's looking for a farm in Virginia. That's kind of a hot thing to do now."

"Connecticut is so yesterday."

"Pricey too."

"I'm sure she can afford it."

"Maybe. But she really does want to get away."

I rest my chin in my hand. "You really think so?"

"Scotty, she's pregnant."

I feel like he's kicked me in the gut. "What?"

"Oh no! Not by me."

"Is she sure?" My skin feels prickly.

"Yes, thank goodness."

I lay my palms flat on the table. "Please don't tell me you've offered to marry her."

He shakes his head. "No. But I did tell her to call me if she finds herself in deep trouble."

"Why?!"

"You got time for a story?"

Dad's at the pastry counter. He'll take all day deciding between the chocolate-chip cookies and the brownies. I know that man. "Yep."

"Okay, after your birthday bash, I went back with Mom and Dad and stayed for a few days. I saw how much they love each other, how Dad takes such good care of Mom with her illness, and how Mom knows how to love my father. She's been taking care of him for years, never really acting like she was doing so, and she forgave him when they split up for a couple of years."

"That's always amazed me."

"Me too. But I was telling her about Karissa and asking her what I should do if Karissa really did want to turn around and needed a friend for moral support."

"I already know the answer."

"Right. Because my mother knows how to love people and forgive them. She made me remember who Jesus really is and what he really taught."

"What are you saying?"

He looks down and reddens. "I guess you could say I remembered who I was when I was in middle school and excited about my faith."

"Really?"

"Yeah, Scotty. I felt so tired of wandering all over the map looking for something I had right with me. I guess you could say I had a revival of sorts."

"Like that tent revival?" I mean, oh no! I can't imagine Seth running around and clapping his hands and speaking in tongues.

"No." He laughs and taps his chest. "In here. It was small and quiet, but I remembered. Scotty"—he takes my hand—"I've forgiven Karissa. And I asked her to forgive me."

"Why?! *You* didn't do—"

"Are you serious? I didn't respect her. I had the chance to be the one guy who treated her with true respect, and I blew it."

I raise my brows. "Well, if you look at it that way . . ."

"I do. So as much as you think she wronged me, it was a two-way deal. I think I owe it to her to be her friend now that she's in such a state. This could just as easily have been my baby." He clears his throat. "Besides, she was planning on having an abortion, and I talked her out of it. I've got to be there for her."

"But aren't you worried you'll fall for her again and it will start all over?"

"Maybe a little. But not really." He squeezes my hand and lets go, and I have no earthly idea what it means, but I wish he'd do it again.

I'm kidding!

Sort of.

Okay, not one bit. But I'm not going to go assuming something and being all stupid. And then there's Angus, who, let's face it, really is way more in my league.

"All right." I sigh. "You're right. And it's the Jesusy thing to do."

"I've got to admit it won't be easy. I'm sure she'll take me up on the offer."

"You don't think you'll have to go into the delivery room with her, do you?"

"Oh, man, I hope not. I can't stand the sight of blood."

"No way!"

"I'm a complete and utter wuss when it comes to all of that."

Oh, Seth.

Jesus, all I can say is you're going to have to protect this guy. Big time.

What about Karissa, Scotty? What about her baby?

I know. I know.

Ninety minutes later

Dad and I hop down from the train.

"Ready to hit the road?"

"No. But let's go anyway."

He holds out his hand, and I place mine inside it. We walk, gripped together, toward the RV, and I'd be lying if I said I wasn't praying that somehow my mother is still alive.

Is that stupid or what? Dad's been trying to find her for years. Who's to say this lead is any good?

"That was a nice time, wasn't it, Dad?"

"Yes."

"I needed that."

"I know you did, honey."

"Thanks."

"You got it."

9:00 p.m.

"Are you sure it's down this road?" I ask.

"Now you're sounding like Grampie."

I laugh. "Well, yeah. But this seems off the beaten path. And The Last Resort? Are you sure this is a reputable campground?"

"I talked with the owner myself, a lady named Helen. She was quite nice."

"If you say so."

I set down my sociology book. I'm getting those electives

in because, baby, I've got one year left, and I am going to college. Dad already said we could travel around this fall and visit schools. But I don't know. It seems like such a big decision, and I'm not ready to even think about it yet, other than dream of sitting in actual classrooms and listening to actual teachers give actual lectures.

The dirt road bumps us toward Long Pond, upon the shores of which The Last Resort nestles. According to the website, there are rustic cabins, and I mean rustic. No indoor toilets. They just added a few RV hookups, so compared to the cabin folk, we'll be living in the lap of luxury.

"Helen told me to allow thirty minutes for the last five miles. I didn't believe her. But I can sure see why now," Dad says.

"At least it's still light enough. Oh look!" I point across a clearing. "A moose! Dad, it's a real moose!"

"My goodness." He stops the RV.

Another one appears, and two more, and they stand there looking our way.

How cool!

We keep watching. None of us moving.

"I think we're in a standoff." Dad laughs.

"Let's let them win. I'm ready to be off the road."

"Me too."

He throws the RV back into drive, and ten minutes later we pull into The Last Resort.

"You know, Dad, you could have picked a place to stay that wasn't so metaphorical."

"Maybe this is the end of the road in our search, Scotty. But maybe it isn't. We might find absolutely nothing."

"I don't believe that."

"Yeah," he sighs. "Me either."

"I just have this feeling."

We hop out of the RV and head into the lodge, a large log cabin about fifty feet from the water. It's twilight, and the water laps softly against a rocky shore. Large pines grow all around, and I like the sound of our heels clonking against the porch boards. Bugs whiz and whir.

A couple sits on an old couch watching television. The woman, skinny from the waist up and plumper down below, hops up. She scrapes thin, graying blonde hair out of her freckled face. "I'm Helen."

"Ezra Dawn."

"Great. Let's get you checked in. That's Jim." She points to her husband, a gray-haired man with glasses and a wise face who's now walking toward us.

We shake his hand. "Glad you made it before it got too dark," he says. "We'll get you set up."

She checks us in, taking Dad's cash and giving him change, telling us the ins and outs. To be honest, she's a little short-speeched, but she's from Maine, so I think it's just her way. Her husband is the kinder, gentler one. I like him.

"Now, to rent a motorboat, it's twenty-five dollars for half a day, forty for a full day, or you can rent it the whole week for a hundred and fifty," she says, "and you have to reserve those. But the canoes are sixty a week, fifteen for the day, three per hour."

"Got it," Dad says, picking up the receipt she's thrust in front of him. "We'll be heading into town a bit. Looking up an old friend. You know the Grobeins?"

Jim joins Helen behind the counter. "Sure. The Grobeins.

Right down the very end of Coburn Avenue near the train tracks?"

"Yep," Dad says.

Jim scratches his cheek. "Now, you know Mrs. Grobein died a few years ago, didn't you?"

"I hadn't heard!"

Oh, Dad. You're really good at this stuff, aren't you?

"She was as old as dirt, but her grandson took good care of her." He turns to his wife. "What's his name, Helen?"

"Don't know him. You're the town socialite, not me."

"Does he still live there?" Dad asks.

"Now that I don't know. I haven't seen him lately if he does. But then, he did always keep to himself. I think his name is Vince."

"Yep, that's it." Helen.

I rub my arms. Vince Grobein is exactly who we're hoping to find. "It's chilly, isn't it?"

"Gets that way sometimes at night." Helen hands us a little campground map that's been recopied so many times it's really just a ghost of its former self. "Jim, why don't you show the Dawns to their site?"

Oh good, I was hoping he'd be the one.

We tromp back to the small parking lot, and Jim hops inside the RV at Dad's invitation. "It'll just be easier than us trying to find it on our own."

He directs us down a dirt road, and we take a right, dipping through a tunnel of pines and into a clearing. And suddenly the world opens up before us. Pines behind and beside us and overhead, stars swimming in an inky sky. Before us, Long Pond catches the stars in its mirrored depths. I suck in my breath. "Wow."

"Pretty, isn't it?"

"Oh yeah," I say.

"Just pull up over there beside the picnic table and mind the fire pit."

Dad glides the TrailMama into its spot and Jim helps him with the hookups as I pick my way down to the lake. I stand on a large, rocky slab that juts out into the water, and joy fills me. I'm here with my father at a cool campground in Maine, and the stars are shining, and soon we'll make a fire, roast our hot-dog dinner, eat our brownie and cheesecake, and I'll fall asleep in my loft with the starlight on my face.

Tuesday, July 12

I awaken to a slight, chilly breeze wafting through the small window in my sleeping loft. The air is cleaner than a razor cut, crisp, and breathes clear, right down to the bottom of my lungs. The secondary smell of the morning? Coffee.

Yes! The man is brilliant.

Dad is nowhere to be seen inside, so I hop down, throw on a robe and open the door. He sits in Charley's blue folding chair by a low-burning campfire, my pink soccer-mom chair opened and waiting for me.

"Good morning, honey." He looks up from the book he's reading. Devotional readings by some guy named Thomas Merton. Don't ask, because I don't know, and I haven't researched him yet, but if his smile on the author photo is any indication, he's nice.

I like nice people.

"Morning, Dad. Good sleep?"

"Yep." He stands up, grabs a potholder off of the picnic table, and lifts the tin coffeepot off the metal fire-pit grid. "Grab a mug."

I step back in and get a mug I bought this summer in Ocean City, Maryland, that says "Maryland Is for Crabs." He fills it up, and soon we're sitting together in the morning sun, the lake sparkling in front of us and sausages sizzling in a grill basket over the hot coals.

I'm just sayin'!

"I'm going to be sad to get off the road someday." I take a sip, and man, my Dad makes great coffee.

"Well, maybe we can take summers and travel around."

"I'd so be up for that."

He turns the grill basket over and sits back down.

"Dad? Do you think it's all behind us? The Mafia? Robertsman?"

Robertsman's running for president. He's a total creep, probably still in the pocket of the Mafia, but he thinks my father died years ago in a shoot-out in Baltimore City.

Bulletproof vests are brilliant.

"As long as we keep our identity hidden, we've got a good chance of staying ahead of the game."

"Will we always have to?"

"Probably. Even if Robertsman has forgotten me, the Mafia hasn't. And they never will. They don't forget anything."

"But don't they think you're dead?"

"Most of them. But . . ." He shakes his head. "Peter will flake out someday. They always do."

Peter is a mobster who found out Dad's still alive. But he's also the one who told Dad that Mom might still be up here with Vince Grobein.

"Drat. This means I'll have to go to college with this name. I'll never get to be Ariana Wethington." You see, I've gotten a little used to the thought of that. I'd go far with a name like that. I can see myself on CNN or with a book on the *New York Times* best-seller list. I might even be some kind of goodwill ambassador with a name like Ariana Wethington.

Dad leans over and jogs my knee. "You're just so Scotty, honey. Do you want to go to college as Ariana?"

"It's a beautiful name."

"Yes, that's why we chose it."

I sigh. "I'd just like it all to be over with, more than anything. I'd like to try a dose of normal. And I'm not complaining about my life, Dad. I'd just like to see what normal's like. Even if I'd end up hating it. At least I'd know."

He looks so sad. "I never knew my life would turn out this way by going into the FBI. I guess I was a little shortsighted."

I grip my mug with both hands. "What would you have done with your life if you hadn't gone into the FBI?"

He laughs. "Honestly?"

"Of course."

"Well, when I was a boy, I loved to build things. I think I'd just like to build things."

"That's pretty general, Dad."

"Yeah. Isn't it great?"

I laugh.

Soon we're eating our sausages with bread Dad toasted over the campfire, drinking our final cups of coffee, both of us steeped in heavy thoughts.

We go about the next thirty minutes in silence, me taking my shower first and getting ready while Dad takes his. It's not a time for music or laughter or chatting.

Family duty calls.

10:00 a.m.

Dad unhitches the pickup truck from the TrailMama, and soon we're on our way back down the dirt road toward town.

"Let's not forget to get some more groceries," he says. "Whatever we find, I think we'll want to stay out the week here. We can rent a canoe and just be together."

"You think she's dead. Don't you? I mean really, Dad."

"I think I'm just preparing myself for the worst."

"Me too. I mean, it just makes sense. *You* found us, right? Why wouldn't she be able to?"

"But your mom wouldn't have the same means I do—*did.*"

"*Do?* Did you just say *do*?"

"Yeah, but all I meant was I'm still in contact with friends at the FBI, still have favors to call in . . ." His words tumble over each other like kids playing leapfrog.

"You're trying to conceal something from me! I know it." I turn in my seat toward him, adjusting my seatbelt to do so. "Come on, Dad. Spill it. You don't have to tell me the ins and outs of your job, but let's face it—your telecommuting and only looking for me on the weekends are two facts that don't add up."

He looks at me and raises an eyebrow. Then he chuckles. "I was wondering how long I could get away with that."

"And what have you been doing now, because you certainly *have* been telecommuting since coming on board with us. So what's the deal?"

The dirt road snakes on before us. Some people put an anti-tourist sign in the yard of their split-foyer home and I am so sure! The Last Resort's website says a camp has been there since 1904. I'd say they were most certainly in the area before some split-foyer home. Correct me if I'm wrong, but split-foyer homes were most definitely not around back then.

Calm down, crazy! Why do you feel so loyal to those folks already? Good grief! I guess my emotions are on high alert.

Dad turns us around a bend and a field of grass stretches before us. Two black dots in the distance begin to move. "More moose!" I say, pointing.

"I suspect we'll see a lot of them."

"I like it. Anyway, as you were saying . . ."

"I wasn't saying anything, honey. I was listening to you hypothesize."

"Oh. But still, you're going to tell me something, right? And why did you disappear that summer after you found me on Ocracoke? You would have been able to locate us through my satellite Internet. That didn't change."

It all becomes so clear!

"Oh all right. But I can only tell you the basics. I'm still with the FBI."

"No! I can't believe it! Tell me it isn't true!"

"I thought you wanted me—"

"Dad! Are we, like, always in danger or something? I mean, is there more to worry about?"

"Well, there's always some degree of risk in my job, but honestly, I'm a technology geek now, honey. And when I was looking for you, I had places I had to be on most Mondays. That summer I was working in DC. Yes, it was computer-geek stuff."

"So you were just fitting my search in on your free time."

"Exactly."

"But after you found me—"

He rounds another curve past some small hunting cabins. "I asked for an extended vacation and then was reassigned to work I could do from here. You wouldn't believe the security on my computer, or my connection."

"You don't use our satellite connection?"

He laughs and laughs.

Okay, it's kinda cool. But not. My dad's been hiding all this from me.

"Why didn't you tell me the whole truth? I'll admit you told me enough to make it kosher, but not everything."

He shrugs, and the road turns to tarmac, and did I tell you it's a sunny day? Just gorgeous. You just want to wrap the sky around you and roll around in some soft grass.

"Honestly, Scotty. You'd been through enough. It was easier for me to have you think I'm just a computer geek. Which basically, honey, is all I am these days."

I lean toward him. "Are you . . . like, a highly talented hacker?"

"Oh brother!" He rolls his eyes. "You'd like to think that, wouldn't you?"

"Are you?"

"Well, if I tell you, I'd have to—"

"What? Kill me?"

He hoots. "No, Miss Dramatic. Probably quit my job or, knowing my luck, get fired."

"Okay. Mum's the word. But I think I guessed it right."

"You're free to think whatever you like. But Scotty, please, never tell a soul."

Dad's asked nothing of me since I've known him. His face is covered in seriousness. "You got it, Dad. I promise."

Twenty minutes later

Hey, this really is a cute town! Older buildings with fresh paint, flowers, and benches; a nice little family restaurant; some other casual eateries; a gift shop — and there's the grocery store we'll hit up after finding Vince. *If* we find Vince.

Dad takes a right onto Coburn Avenue. Yep, just like the map said, there are train tracks to our left, and small houses line the street. At the very end, two houses face one another on the opposite sides of the road. One is a small white frame house, minimalist when it comes to shrubbery. In other words, there are no shrubs at all. Across the street, a mustard-yellow house sits amid so many lawn ornaments: gnomes (naturally), reflecting balls (of course), and at least ten hooks bearing hanging baskets or wind chimes.

"I can't imagine Babette at either of these places." Dad shakes his head. "The one's too plain and the other too . . . too . . ."

"Corny?"

"Yes. That would be the right word."

He parks at the dead end of the street.

"I like it though, Dad. It looks like somebody nice lives there. Somebody who hopes the neighbor across the street will enjoy the flowers and all the flash."

Dad eyes the plain house. "If he does, he's crazy."

"Maybe you're right about that."

He places his hand on his door handle. "Ready?"

I reach for my purse. "Gotta be."

"Let's go."

"Grobein," Dad says, taking my hand. "Which one is your guess?"

"Sounds like a German name."

"Let's go with the plain one."

"Okay. But I really hope it's the other one."

Dad winks. "I do too. Makes it seem like Vince turned out to be a really nice guy."

"Or he's trying to convince the neighbors he is."

"I like the way you think, missy!"

We step up onto the curb and the walkway leading up to the porch. No rocking chairs or tables rest on the floorboards, painted a shiny battleship gray.

"Dad?" I stop.

"What is it, honey?"

"Do I look okay?"

He turns to me, his face dissolving into a loving mush. "Oh, Scotty, you look beautiful."

"Because if Mom's there, I want her to be proud of me. To think I turned out well. That . . . well, I guess I want her to think I'm pretty."

He puts his arms around me. "You are, honey. Inside and out. Any woman would be proud to call you her daughter. But your mother, she especially would. She would love that outfit."

A longish, seventies-looking brown skirt with embroidery around the hem that Grammie and I made flows beneath my poet shirt. A long string of bronze pearls is wrapped once around my throat, the rest hanging down to my stomach. Bronze leather flip-flops anchor me to the pavement. Hair in a French twist. Bronze lipstick.

"Are you sure? Does it look like I'm trying too hard?"

"No. You look like you. And that's a wonderful thing."

I squeeze him tight, and he lets me go. We continue up the steps to stand before the white front door.

Dad reaches out and rings the bell.

We wait.

The wind blows, the sun shines, the smell of fresh-cut grass fills the air as if all is normal today. I look down at my hands clasped in front of me and want to scream, it seems like it's taking so long. Then I hear footsteps from inside. I breathe deeply. Okay, Jesus, here we go. Is this it? The end of a long journey? Or is another one just beginning?

An unseen hand turns the brass knob, and the door swings open wide. Before us stands a teenage boy.

Shoot. I was so not expecting this.

His brows knit, scrunching together a plain face with snappish eyes. "Yeah?"

Dad steps forward. "We're looking for the Grobeins."

"Mrs. Grobein is dead."

"I understand that. Do you know the whereabouts of her grandson?"

"V? Sure. Lives across the street. But I wouldn't go over there if I were you."

"Why?" I ask.

"Been a recluse since his grandmother died." He leans forward. "The guy actually mows his lawn at night. Hand mower."

Hand mower? What's he mean?

Dad turns to me. "The nonelectric kind with the spinning blades."

"Got it." I nod.

"Oh well, thank you. Sorry to disturb you."

"'Bye," I say.

"See ya." He starts to shut the door.

"One more thing," Dad says.

"Yeah?"

"Does he have anybody else living with him? A woman or anyone?"

The guy shakes his head. "Not that I've ever seen, and we've lived here for about three years."

"Thank you, then."

He closes the door completely.

I hurry off the porch and head to the sidewalk, then I turn. "What do you make of this?"

"Too soon to jump to conclusions, Scotty. Let's just go knock on his door and see what happens."

"He's not gonna like it."

"Maybe not. But I'm not too concerned about him right now, to tell you the truth."

Gosh, I love my dad.

We cross the street, head up onto the porch and once again stand in front of a stranger's domain.

No doorbell. Dad opens the screen and knocks on the red front door.

No answer.

He knocks again.

We wait.

The wind still blows, the sun still shines, the air still smells like mown grass, and I've got even more questions than I did before.

Nothing.

"He's not going to answer." Dad quietly shuts the screen door.

"I kinda suspected that." A piece of hair falls into my eyes, and I shove it back. "What are we going to do?"

Dad eyes the lawn. "Grass needs cutting. We're just going to have to wait until dark."

"Here? On this porch?"

"No, silly. We'll come back later."

"Will he come out with our truck parked right here?"

Dad laughs, takes my arm, and ushers me toward the truck. "Okay, Scotty, think for a minute. Who am I?"

"Oh."

"So if you were me, what would the plan be?"

"Park farther on down the street and wait there."

"Precisely."

"So we'll arrive here at dusk or so?"

"Yes. That's exactly what we'll do."

Ten minutes later

Dad pushes the cart down the aisles of the Mountain Country Store, a local no-frills grocery. But they have a deli, and he promised me we could get some broasted chicken. Love that broasted chicken.

"I figure we'd better not have anything too heavy on our stomachs tonight with what lies ahead. How about chicken and dumplings?" He reaches down to the bottom shelf for a small box of Bisquick.

"Good idea."

I'm not going to say anything, but chicken and dumplings isn't exactly green salad and quiche.

We stock up on soda, chips, and hot dogs. A couple of steaks and some chicken breasts for the rest of the week. "Let's cook over the campfire as much as we can," he says.

"Most definitely."

Some grapes, apples, and kiwi fruit, fresh veggies, eggs, bacon, bread, and deli roast beef, Muenster, provolone, butter, mayo, pickles, and we are out the door.

We eat our broasted chicken in the car, breaking into the crispy skin with our teeth, the hot juices bursting forth. This is just about the most brilliant thing you can put into your mouth. I'm just sayin'.

I'm wiping my mouth and throwing my napkins into the take-out box when the cell phone rings.

I look at the number. "It's Charley." I flip open the phone. "Hi, Charley!"

"Hi, baby!"

"How's Scotland?"

"It's more than groovy. In fact, I don't think *groovy* begins to cover it. Oh, baby, it's so beautiful here." Her voice is light, airy, and clear. Happiness fills every syllable.

"And Harris?" Anthony Harris is the most humble famous person I have ever met. And I've met my share.

"Just who I expected him to be. He's even more wonderful in his own environment."

"So tell me everything."

My smile grows as she describes Harris's castle. While not a super-large castle, it's old, old, old but has its modern spaces inside. There's a great kitchen, and she's already made a wonderful meal from the vegetables grown on the organic farm Harris runs. They even make their own cheeses, and she's beginning to rethink the evils of dairy products. (Hallelujah!) His housekeeper's a gem, Scottish, of course, with three young children who are always running around the place. Oh, and he's got a suit of armor. A real suit of armor, not one of those fake things you see at flea markets.

"Any ghosts about the place?"

"Not that I can tell. Oh, and I met Tony's pastor. He came for dinner last night. I loved him. I've got to tell you, baby, if I'd had a pastor like him when I was young, I might be in a different place now."

"Hey, pretend you are young and soak it in for all it's worth!"

"You know, that's a good attitude."

I mean Jesus said to come to him as a little child, right? Here's hoping Charley can find some peace and the knowledge that she can put her past behind her and find life, a good life.

"Tell Harris I said hi!"

"I will. He said to give you his regards and that he fully expects you to come visit with me next time."

Like there's going to be another visit for Charley. She's going to stay there. I just know it.

"So how long are you planning on staying?"

"I don't know. As long as it feels right."

See? She's toast.

I like it.

7:00 p.m.

We unloaded groceries, sat by the water in the soccer moms, and read all afternoon. I now think of that big smooth rock as my own and yes, it's better than the bottom of a swimming pool. *Lady Oracle* behind me, and good riddance, I'm well into the first half of *The Sun Also Rises* by Hemingway. Angus swears it's his favorite book.

Dad made up the chicken and dumplings, both of us just sort of picking at it when dinnertime rolled around.

So now we do the dishes together. I fill the sink with water, the suds from the dishwashing liquid building beneath the stream of warm water.

"Dad? What are we going to do with our lives from here on out? Charley's not coming back. We both know it. And whether we find Mom or not, we still have to plan a life. What about moving to Delaware near Grammie and Grampie?"

"I can't afford to live there, honey."

"Yeah, I know. I guess maybe, now that I think about it, I'm asking a bigger question. It's really a broader question. What do we want to be about, you and me?"

"What do you mean?"

"Well, take my new friend Megan for instance. She's totally giving her life to God, taking care of those children and all. I mean, don't you ever feel like you'd like your life to be really extraordinary?"

"I thought it was." He sets the dish rack on the counter.

"It is. Don't get me wrong. But I don't mean investigator extraordinary. I mean Jesusy extraordinary."

He nods. "I guess I do. It's hard to think about your life in those terms, though, isn't it? Or maybe a little frightening to lay it all down like that."

"I guess." I slide our plates, utensils, and cups into the soapy water. "Dad, I just don't want to get to the end of the road and think I really didn't do anything to actually help out in the world."

"It's a good thing to think about."

I scrub a plate. "Frustrating, though. I just don't know how to go about it." I rinse the plate and set it in the drain board.

He picks up the dish and begins to dry. "Tell you what. Why don't you commit to praying about it? I mean really praying."

"It's definitely a prayer God will answer. I mean, he doesn't hide himself from view when you really want to do his work, does he?"

"I don't know, honey. But I'm sure he'll want you to talk to him about it."

"You're right."

After we finish, I head down to my rock and I talk to God, the shadows of the trees behind me lengthening, swallowing me and the shoreline as they grow.

I just simply tell God what's going on in my heart as the birds fly around me and the mosquitoes start to bite. And I feel like God's listening because he promised he would.

Do you want to be like Jesus, Scotty?

The words fill my brain.

"Is that where I start, Lord?" I say the words out loud.

I remember Jesus telling his disciples he was the Way. Oh! So that's what that means.

Okay then, Jesus. Show me what to do.

The first step, I realize, is forgiving the Karissa, even though she'd never ask me to.

I sigh. This'll be a hard one. So I give it a practice run.

"I forgive you," I whisper. "For all the put downs and the way you led Seth down a bad path. But I forgive you because I have to. And even if I don't feel it like I probably should, I'm just deciding to do it anyway."

Jesusy extraordinary. I mean, he forgave the whole world. Right?

10:00 p.m.

We're about five houses down from Vince's place. Or V as that kid called him. Dad found out earlier this year that Vince, after my mom was kidnapped by the Mafia, ran off with her. He must have fallen in love with her, because who wouldn't? Babette was that kind of woman.

Dad peers through a set of tiny binoculars and has opened our windows so we can hear if Vince starts clipping away at that lawn.

"The light in the living room just went on. I imagine he'll have to move some of those lawn ornaments first if he's planning to mow." Dad takes a sip from a water bottle. "That will take a while."

"Maybe we can walk by, pretending we're new in town, and offer to lend a hand."

"Good idea. Actually, I'll go by myself, honey. We don't know his mental state, and I'm not going to put you in harm's way."

"Drat."

"Thanks for not arguing."

"Oh please, Dad. Don't you hate it in movies when the pro has to take some bumbling idiot along, usually a woman, I might add, who's going to mess up the works because she's too loud or can't run fast enough? They totally put it in so they can keep the two stars together. It's the most hackneyed device in the movies." I think for a second or two. "Other than when they all put their hands together and do the team thingee. I hate that too. But at least it's not so sexist."

"So tell me how you really feel, honey." He laughs and takes my hand.

"You'll be all right, won't you, Dad?"

"Scotty, I know how to do this. I doubt Vince will be careless here on his street. He's hidden himself from his past for years. He won't take that lightly."

I sigh. "I sure hope you're right. What if he doesn't come out?"

"We'll be sitting back here tomorrow night."

"Are you packing?"

"A gun?"

"Well, yeah."

"Would I tell you if I were?"

"Nope." I pause. "So are you?"

"Nope."

"It's a sin to lie, Dad."

"Scotty, stop."

"Okay, okay."

Later

I jerk awake. "Dad?"

"It's midnight, honey. Let's go back to camp."

"He didn't come out."

"I knocked on his door, but no answer."

"As we would expect."

"Precisely."

Wednesday, July 13, 8:00 a.m.

I check my e-mail. Violette Dillinger wrote. Cool.

> Scotty,
> Still lovin' the website, babe. Was wondering if you could update the picture on the front. File attached. Thanks!
> BTW, I'm back with Joe and things are better than ever. Do you think eighteen is too young to get married?
> Vi

Oh, my goodness. How do I know? People used to get married young all the time, but then careers started happening for women. But Violette already has a good career going.

This question is so out of my league it isn't even funny.

And "babe?" Where did that come from?

I click on Reply.

> Vi,
> Will do with the pic. Nice, by the way. I really like it. As for your other question, there have to be far more qualified people to ask. I'm just trying to get through high school! <g>
> Scotty

7:00 p.m.

Dad and I clean up the dishes again after another afternoon on the rock. Steak and salad tonight.

"Ready to try again?" he asks.

"Yep."

He sets the final dish in the cupboard and folds the dishtowel. "You know, it could take a while. I remember one time sitting in a van for two months."

"Oh, man. Do you really think it'll take that long? And does The Last Resort even have openings for that long?"

"No and no. He'll have to mow his lawn soon."

"It looks like he takes care of his lawn regularly."

"And it's looking a little scraggly. You have to keep up on things with those hand mowers too. If the grass gets too thick, it's almost impossible."

"If you say so."

Are we just talking ourselves into something that's simply not going to happen? I don't know. But we've got to keep it up. That I do know.

11:00 p.m.

Another fruitless evening and Vince's grass grows ever longer.

"Let's go then, honey. Apparently not tonight, either."

"Nope. I guess not."

11:45 p.m.

We sit out under the stars, a small campfire glowing, neither of us ready to settle down and sleep.

"I feel so . . . tentative," I tell Dad. "Like that feeling you get in a disaster movie because you've seen the trailer. So the earthquake's coming, and all is quiet. The animals go nuts, then get still."

"That pretty much describes it, honey."

"I don't even feel like reading."

"Me either."

"Hold on a second."

I run into the RV and bring out my CD player. I punch play, and the tones of Beethoven's *Moonlight* Sonata softly fill the space. "That's it, Dad. That song. It's exactly how I feel."

"The old guy nailed it."

"Yes. Yes, he did."

We listen until the final note drifts over the lake.

"Now put that thing away and pluck a little on that harp. I could use a little of that."

I sit on the picnic table bench, the harp resting between my legs, and I pluck the few tunes I know: "Barbara Allen," "Greensleeves," "My Heart's in the Highlands," and "Amazing Grace."

Even the most simple tunes on a harp are beautiful enough to make your heart expand.

"Dad, I want my life to be beautiful too."

"It already is, Scotty."

"No, I mean, like I want to do beautiful things with my life."

An hour later, when we get ready for bed, I check my cell phone. A text came in from Seth.

Seth: Bck in Delawre at the nw house. safe and sound. newfnd celibacy intct.

I bark out a laugh.

"What is it?" Dad.

"Just Seth being funny."

But it's not funny. Not really. It's brave. And I'm proud of him. Jesus, let's pray he can keep the resolve in Hollywood. I mean Delaware and Hollywood are about as far away from each other as Mercury and the used-to-be-planet Pluto.

Me: Good for you. I'm just heading to bed. I'll text you tomorrow.

It's late, and I have a lot of rolling around trying to sleep to accomplish before the morning light.

Thursday, July 14, 9:30 p.m.

"There he is," Dad whispers. "He's moving the lawn ornaments now."

"Okay. I'll be watching with the binoculars."

"I'll give you the sign if everything's okay. Then come on over."

I nod. "Got it."

He leans forward and kisses me on the forehead. "Love you, honey. Sit tight."

He's kissing me good-bye, just in case. I know this. "Oh, Dad.

Maybe we shouldn't take the chance. I mean, he might feel threatened and pull out a gun or something. Anything could happen."

"I'll be all right."

He looks cooler than any cucumber I've ever seen, and growing up with Charley the Ditzy Vegan, I've seen a lot of cucumbers.

"Promise me you'll be all right."

"I've gotta go while he's still out."

I don't ask for a promise again, not one he absolutely can't make. It's not one any of us can really make, not if we believe we're in God's hands and he's allowed to do what he wants as long as it doesn't conflict with his love for us. My wise friend Maisie told me that online in the Christian RV chatroom a few weeks ago.

I kiss him on the cheek. "Be careful. I'll be watching."

"Will do."

The door latch releasing is loud and echoey, like a sound effect some Foley artist put into a movie during post-production. The sound of him sliding off the vinyl seat grates my ears, and when he shuts the door, though he does so quietly, it's like a bomb has gone off. Oh, Dad.

Wait! I want to scream the words, but I can't. I have to trust him right now. I have to believe he knows what he's doing. I have to believe he'll do the right thing. I have to believe God will take care of him one way or the other. I have to believe God will take care of me in exactly the same manner.

Oh yes, it all sounds so holy, Jesus, but you and I both know that God lets really bad things happen to people all the time.

The darkness swallows all of him except for his white T-shirt, the one Violette sent him that says, "Pavlov: the name rings a bell."

I slide into the driver's seat and hold the binoculars up to my eyes.

Breathe, Scotty. Don't forget to breathe.

The seconds ooze by like he's caught in some slow-motion beam somebody's aiming at him from overhead. One foot in front of the other, hands in his pockets. Past one house. Past the second house. Past the third. Until . . .

He stops and begins to chat. I can't hear a word they're saying, of course, and I'm dying to. Why couldn't we be wired up professionally right now—Dad with a small mic taped in his cap, me listening on the other end to hear it all?

No. We're small potatoes.

But not that small. I mean, God sees us. And if there is ever a time to pray, now is it. But I can't concentrate on the words, so I dedicate everything I'm feeling in my heart, all the words swimming in my brain, all the fears swimming behind my eyes, I dedicate them all in prayer, confident God will arrange them in a cohesive order.

The conversation lingers. For one minute. Two. Then Dad turns on his heel and walks toward the truck. No signal. No signs. Just Dad coming back to the truck. Safe. Unharmed.

As he steps into a lighted pool from a nearby streetlamp, I see the paleness of his skin, the look of one stunned by the worst of news, and I know she's dead.

My mother is dead.

Thirty seconds later

Dad wipes his forehead with a bandana and opens up the door.

"What happened, Dad?"

He slides in. "Your mom's not there. I tried to get him to tell me where she is, but he wouldn't."

"Did he claim to know her?"

He shakes his head. "No. Shoot, Scotty, I don't know why Vince would admit something straight up to a stranger. It's not his MO, and I don't blame him."

"Was he hostile?"

"*Guarded* would be a more accurate description."

"Did he recognize you?"

"If he did, he hid it well. I can't tell you. He's a pro, honey, not likely to show his hand."

I sigh. "So . . . she's not there."

"No. I don't think so anyway. That kid would have said something if she lived there. At least I think so."

"Could he be keeping her prisoner? Like he's had her locked up for years or something?"

"This isn't the movies, Scotty."

I close my eyes against the beam from the streetlamp. This can mean so many things. For one, she's dead. For two, she escaped him and he doesn't know where she is, which means . . . for three, this search is long from over.

"I just want this to be over," I say. "One way or the other."

"Me too, Scotty. I'm sorry."

"I shouldn't have gotten my hopes up. I mean, I didn't think

I had until you came walking back to the car with that look on your face."

He turns to me and places his hand on my shoulder. "Honey, how could you have done otherwise?" He leans in. "Truthfully, I guess I had my hopes up too."

I smile with one side of my mouth. "Then we're in the same boat."

He nods. "That is something you can safely say no matter what."

What would I do without my dad, you ask? I don't know. I went for so long without him, not thinking I needed him. But I did. Oh I did.

He starts up the engine. "I gave him my phone number and told him where we were staying in case he changes his mind. He took the number."

"Well, that's encouraging. I mean, he would have refused if he really wasn't Vince or something."

"Oh, it was Vince. I know that for sure."

"Yeah. I guess he didn't get all tattooed up like you did."

He begins a three-point turn in the middle of the street. "You're exactly right."

And we head back to The Last Resort.

Saturday, July 16, 2:00 p.m.

Dad guides the TrailMama over the lovely ribbon of concrete curling along the eastern seaboard toward Delaware. We stayed another day in Maine, though it appeared Vince left home after Dad's visit.

Dad chatted it up with some of the other neighbors along the street, and one lady remembered a woman there with Vince, but that was a long time ago, she said. She remembered an ambulance once as well.

"You know," I say, setting my pen down along the crease of Elaine, my journal. "I just wish I had one memory of Mom. Just one real memory. But there's nothing."

"I'm sorry about that, Scotty."

"I mean, I love hearing you tell me things, don't get me wrong. I love hearing about how much she loved me and the way she cared for me, the things she did; but, Dad, I just want something real. Something to hold on to." I swallow. "Whether she's alive or not."

Dad pulls up to a tollbooth. "You know I'd do anything for you Scotty" — he pays the operator — "but some things I just can't. And this is something I wish I *could* do. I can't tell you how much I want for you to be able to remember your mother like I do."

He glides on through, only to come to a stop fifteen seconds later. Traffic on Saturdays during the summer is terrible in these parts. I sure wouldn't want to live around here and have to deal with this week after week.

Hmm. There's a lesson in that, isn't there?

Dad shifts lanes easily despite the size of the RV and the truck dangling off the back, and I wonder about him and others like him who love the dangerous life, who take chances in ways most men, no matter how macho they are, would never consider.

Maybe, somewhere down deep inside, he's a little crazy. Maybe that craziness led him to be an agent with the FBI. And maybe, when you really come down to it, all this really is his fault.

He turns to me and smiles, all his hopes for me, all the love he feels contained inside. And I smile back, pick up the pen, and write on Elaine's lines:

Dear Elaine,

Today I chose to "not go there." I won't blame my dad for any of this even if he could have chosen differently somewhere along the path. It doesn't matter now. Whatever happened to Babette has happened. The whys aren't important other than as clues to the truth. The truth is, my father loves me and he's human and he's not always going to make the safe choice, or even the one that makes sense to most people. But that's okay. I'd rather take him as he is than not to have him at all. Because I know what that was like, and it wasn't good.

"So what's next?" I ask, closing Elaine and dropping her onto the floorboard. "Do we keep searching for Mom?"

"I don't know. My instincts are telling me to wait awhile. You should go on to Kentucky to the children's home, and maybe something will develop. Vince has my number."

"Maybe he'll have a change of heart."

"Maybe."

But I can hear the rest of the sentence left silent. *But don't count on it.*

Why can't life ever be neat and tidy?

Tuesday, July 19, 9:30 a.m.

Okeydokey. The soccer mom is set up in the sand, and I'm making my list for my trip. I leave on Thursday for Kentucky and the children's home. Megan says they moved an extra bed for me into her room and insists she doesn't mind at all, giving me the "Oh, it'll be fun to have a little sister for a month" spiel. Whether it's true remains to be seen, but I can tell you this: I'm going to try to be a really nice little sister not a bratty one. I want to soak in every moment because I'm thinking in one of those moments I just might hear God speak to me.

So here's what I've got so far:

2 pairs of jeans
2 pairs of shorts
2 cool skirts
5 shirts
5 T-shirts
underpants
bras
socks
boxers and tanks

slippers
robe
sneakers
flip-flops
sandals
sweatshirt
jacket
soccer mom
Elaine
harp
computer
F. Scott Fitzgerald collection
toiletries
notepads
pens

So far so good. And good thing Dad has a pickup truck, with all this stuff!

I stare off into the ocean, the gray breakers of midafternoon depositing white foam onto the beige sand. Over and over they come, like God's clock, bringing life onto the shore with each crash. Gentle waves today.

"Hey, you."

I turn. "Seth! What are you doing here? I thought you went back up to New York."

"I finished up yesterday"—he approaches with two soda cans in one hand—"and thought I'd come here for a day or two before heading back to LA. Can I sit?"

"Most definitely."

He hands me a Coke, crouches down next to me, and settles

himself in the sand. He's wearing frayed jeans, no shoes, and a dark green T-shirt that says "Disguised as an Adult" in yellow letters.

I poke his shoulder. "Well, if you'd have worn that shirt a few months ago, I'd have agreed completely. But you seem to be doing better now."

"You never change." He laughs and flips the top on his 7-Up. "Thank goodness."

"So what's next in LA?"

"A romantic comedy with Diane Keaton."

"Whoa. That'll be cool."

"Yeah. Then some voice work for a DreamWorks production, and after that I'll be off until after Christmas."

"You coming back here?"

"Absolutely."

"Seth, when's Karissa's baby due?"

He sets down his can, twisting it into the sand to hold it upright. "Nice forewarning."

"Sorry. I've just been wondering."

"March. Sometime near the beginning, I think."

A plane flies just off the shoreline. It's trailing a banner advertising a prime-rib special at The Bonfire down in Ocean City.

"What's she going to do in the meantime?"

"She's got her latest film releasing next week, so she's doing a publicity tour and then she's taking a break. I'm worried about her."

"I'll bet."

He looks out at the ocean. "No really, Scotty. She's still drinking. I'm hoping she's not doing drugs, but I can't be sure. Somebody's got to reach out to her. We're planning on meeting for lunch once I get back. I wanted to be up front about that."

"You don't have to explain yourself to me, Seth."

He laughs. "Oh yeah, right, Scotty!"

Okay, I see his point. "Sorry."

"No! No, it's good for me. I don't know where I'd be right now without you standing there with your arms crossed, looking at me beneath furrowed brow."

"True." I sip my drink. "Nice on the 'furrowed brow' bit, by the way."

"She called me, crying. She doesn't want to live like this. She knows she's wrong. She's begging for my help. But the thing is, when I get out there I'll be so busy, I don't know how much help I'll be."

"Oh, Seth, please. You'll spend every spare minute trying to get her back on track. You know it."

"You're probably right," he says with a sigh. "What a mess."

Here's my question: Is sex so great, I mean really so, so, so great that it's worth risking it all for? Risk pregnancy and all sorts of creepy diseases (not to mention diseases that will kill you)? Or are they really looking for something else? I have no clue, and I'm fine keeping it that way, to tell you the truth.

So here's the deal. Karissa needs a dose of reality. She's doing stupid stuff to her baby when there are people everywhere who are dying to have a baby, and children at homes like Megan's who need moms. Yeah, yeah. I need a dose of reality too. But at least I don't have an innocent person riding on my reality check. And I've got Dad and all the people who love me supporting me.

"Get her to come to Kentucky with me."

Oh, my gosh. What am I saying? This is the most ridiculous thing I've ever said in my entire life. Am I insane?

"I doubt she'll take you up on it. I know Karissa pretty well. I can't imagine her doing something like that."

Phew. "Yeah. I figured."

A beach ball rolls up to Seth's feet. He pitches it back to a little boy in a bright red bathing suit. "Here you go, bud!" He turns back to me. "I'll mention it to her though. I mean, you never know."

"People have done stranger things, right?"

My phone rings. Angus!

"Hey, Angus!"

"Hi, Scotty. Just checkin' in to see how you are."

"Leaving soon for Kentucky. How're things in Richmond?"

Seth whispers, "Who's Angus again?"

I snort silently and listen to Angus.

"They're fine. My sister got a boyfriend, so that keeps her mind off the divorce. And speaking of boyfriends, I was wondering about that trip up to see you."

Uh . . . boyfriend?

So okay, I'm sitting here with Angus in one ear and Seth by the other and . . . boyfriend?

Oh, that's right. I'm Seth's little sister. That's right.

"Why don't you come up after I get back from Kentucky?"

"That'd be great. Hey, gotta get to work. Just wanted to see how you were."

"Thanks, Angus. August will be brilliant."

"Looking forward to it."

We hang up.

"That guy from Asheville?" Seth asks.

"Yep."

"Is he good-looking?"

"Seth, you know me better than to think that's the main thing I look for in a guy."

"True."

"But yeah, he's good-looking, in a unique sort of way. Not your typical Hol—" Oh crap, why did I say that?

"Typical Hollywood good-looking?" He laughs. "Scotty, you're a trip."

"Hey, I'm unique."

"You said it."

Another plane flies by. Seth points to it. "How about sharing one of those pizzas at the Dough Roller tonight?"

"Sure."

Pizza and Seth Haas. Not a bad combination, especially considering the pizza is loaded with cheese.

Am I wrong in thinking he wouldn't have asked me to go get pizza if Angus hadn't called?

"And did you actually use the word *brilliant*, Scotty?"

"Yeah. You like? I'm just trying it on for size."

"Veddy veddy British."

"Veddy. I figure if Anthony Harris is going to be part of our lives, I might as well do a little importing beforehand."

"You crack me up."

He pulls a small paperback out of his back pocket, I pull one out of my beach bag, and we settle in for some reading.

I like it.

6:00 p.m.

Seth pulls up to Grammie and Grampie's house in his new East Coast car, as he calls it. Oh brother. But whatevs. An old Triumph Spitfire. Yes, it's cool, almost as cool as his beach bungalow, a modern, low-slung house with a wall of glass facing the ocean, just north of Bethany Beach.

Grammie hands me one of her head scarves, a groovy piece of silk in bright colors. "You'll need this. Trust me."

The sun still shines when I climb in, and I place sunglasses on my nose.

"You look so Audrey Hepburn." Seth sets his own glasses on his nose.

"Thanks."

"You know, Scotty, you're really pretty. You've changed a lot over the past year and a half."

"Nice of you to notice."

Downright brilliant.

Calm down, Scotty. He's still three years older than you are. Okay, four.

Wednesday, July 20, 2:00 p.m.

My last day on the beach before heading to the mountains. I've slathered on one million SPF sunscreen, jammed one of Grammie's cool straw hats on my head, and I'm sure I'll still be fried tomorrow. But I don't care. I just want to soak this all in before heading back to the house and the big going-away dinner Grammie and Grampie are making. Grampie's famous mixed grill, coming right up.

I've finished my literature course through Indiana University High School, as well as Algebra 2, science, and sociology, and I'm taking a break until I get back from Megan's.

Got a funny card from Angus and a newsy letter from Joy Overstreet, a sweet designer I met in the Outer Banks last summer. She's moved to New York and met a guy, a nice man who owns a candy shop. Down in Texas, my friend Grace and her baby May are still doing great, and yes, Jacob the coffee-shop owner popped the question to Phoebe the drama teacher, and they're planning a Christmas wedding. Jeanne's going to sing, and her husband will accompany her on the guitar. The ladies from the Design Center are taking care of the decorations. They'll do a great job. And the coolest part? They're redoing that fabulous old Elks Lodge into a killer apartment complex. Man, I hope I can go back to Marshall someday to see them all.

Last night's dinner with Seth has made me a little dreamy. One teenage girl asked him for his autograph, and he was so sweet about it. When her mother admonished her, he said, "No, ma'am, it's okay. I really don't mind one bit."

Wait until he's *really* famous.

There at the beach, I open up Elaine and begin to write.

Dear Elaine,
So I know I was crushing a little bit on Angus, but I have to be honest with you of all people that my heart belongs to Seth. It's

crazy and it's creepy, and I've got as much chance with him as I do of plummeting over Niagara Falls in a barrel. Actually, I've got way more chances with the barrel.

It's hopeless. Truly. But now that he's got his act together again, I remember why I came to care for him so much back on Toledo Island when I first met him. He was so nice then. And he's so nice now.

Is he really over the Karissa? I guess time will tell.

I guess a part of me hopes that someday he'll see me in a romantic light, but think of all the women he'll meet before then. Beautiful, successful actresses, not to mention women just throwing themselves at him. And I can't say all of them will be skanky broads. Some might be lovely and lonely and as nice as he is. So I don't know. I'm silly, I guess.

And he's lived a far less sheltered life than I have. Maybe, even if he did come to care for me in that way, he'd figure somebody like me, without experience in all sorts of ways, wouldn't have him.

Hmm. Well, maybe there is somebody else for me. But I guess I'm just not willing to hold his mistakes against him. Not when he's come so far. I don't know. It's not easy. These thoughts feel so confusing. Even Jesus said he didn't come to call the righteous to repentance, but sinners. If Jesus accepts Seth, who am I not to?

Like it's even going to happen! I'm an idiot for even entertaining these thoughts. What in the world would Seth, a Hollywood hottie, see in a nobody like me?

There, that depressed me enough for a good week's worth of downer feelings. But I remind myself that nothing about my life has changed since I sat down in this chair three hours ago. Not one thing. I'm firmly committed to not going emo.

I'm *definitely* just sayin'.

Families and couples are spread out before me in this busy beach season. Radios play. Kids play. And the beach walkers traipse across the hardened sand by the surf. An old couple walks by, hand in hand, laughing and so easy with each other. That's the kind of couple, like Grammie and Grampie, I want to be part of someday when I'm old. I just love old people.

Speaking of old people, I wonder how good old Bob and Doris are? Which son's or daughter's driveway holds their Happy Couple RV right now? I've got to send them an e-mail when I get back to the house.

My cell phone rings.

"Charley!"

"Baby!"

"How's Scotland and your hottie boyfriend?"

I swear I can see her rosy, flaming blush from across the ocean. Nice.

"He's fine."

"I'm almost all packed for Kentucky. We're heading down there tomorrow."

"That's great. I'm so proud of you, Scotty."

"Well, I haven't done anything yet."

"But you want to. And I think that's pretty extraordinary."

Jesusy extraordinary? Well, that will remain to be seen, because Jesus, you know I can be a real jerk sometimes. I mean, what if there's someone who works there who's a size 0, uses a straightening iron and always has lip gloss on?

I'm just sayin'!

An hour later

Angus sends me a picture by text. Aww man. He really is cute, and he's yet to make big-time mistakes like Seth.

Thursday, July 21, 10:00 a.m.

Dad and I have been on the road for a few hours now. Last night we had a great dinner with Grammie, Grampie, and Seth, who brought along a big case of Coke for me to take south.

He kissed me on the cheek when he left and didn't call me little sis like he usually does. But don't get me wrong. It was a brotherly kiss. Nothing romantic about it.

At least he thinks I'm prettier than I used to be.

I'll take it.

We're just through Cumberland, Maryland, when a text message arrives.

Seth: Krssa wnts 2 tlk about the orphnge.

Me: You're kidding me!

Seth: No. i clled hr lst nght and tld hr about it. it took some convncng 4 hr 2 evn agree 2 lt u cll hr.

Me: But I don't know a whole lot about it yet.

Seth: Heres hr cll phn nmbr.

And there it sits. In all its glory. All those numbers just lined up in a neat little row. The Karissa's sought-after cell phone number. I could sell it for big bucks. Big bucks I tell you.

But I won't.

I mean, I don't like the girl much, but please. That's all she would need at a time like this. There's the baby to think about now.

Oh, man! I do have to call her, don't I? This is decidedly *not* brilliant.

Okay, Jesus. But is this what making a difference in people's lives really means? I was talking about poor people, sad and lonely people who can't help themselves. Old people, sick people, disabled people, little kids. Not rich, spoiled movie stars. And remember that rich young ruler that went away sad because you told him to sell all his possessions and give them to the poor? What about him?

I know, I know. Who am I to be so choosy?

I know what I have to do, but this stinks. Can I at least say that?

Me: Okay, I'll give her a call. You be careful at lunch with her, Seth.

Seth: I wll. blve me I wll. u b crful on th road.

Me: Will do. Bye Seth.

Seth: C ya Sctty.

Great, just great. Me and my big mouth. I stop blogging to get away from thinking about stupid stars like the Karissa and what happens? The Karissa ends up coming to me. This stinks.

Oh yeah. I said that already.

But it still applies, and I have a feeling it's going to apply for a good long time. Unless she doesn't come. Please Jesus, don't let her come.

Okay, even I know that was an utterly lousy thing to pray for. I take it back.

Yeah, you knew I would. I know, I know.

"Dad?"

"Yeah, honey?"

"I need to make a private phone call."

"What's up?"

I explain the situation.

He whistles between his teeth. "Oh, honey. My goodness. What have you gotten yourself into this time?"

"Clearly something I'm incapable of handling."

He shrugs. "I don't know. You never know what will happen with crazy sorts of things."

Yeah, you never know.

"I'll pull off at the next exit. I could use a cup of coffee."

Okay.

We pull into a gas station with a mini-mart, and I hop out. Around the side of the building, near the Dumpster (how fitting), I dial the number. Let's see. It's around ten thirty here, so that makes it seven thirty her time.

I smile. Oh, this is perfect. She'll hang up right away it's so early. Her hangover is probably thicker than Pam Anderson's makeup. And she's way more likely to say no.

But there's a real little person growing inside of her. And why do you keep reminding me of that, Jesus?

Yes, your own mother was unmarried and pregnant. I get that. But, correct me if I'm wrong, the circumstances of your conception were markedly different.

I punch in the number and to be honest, I feel a little sick to my stomach. It rings four times, and I'm thinking the message will kick in soon. What will it say?

"It's Karissa. Leave a message."

"I'm hot. Are you? If so, leave a message."

"Nobodies like Scotty need not apply. Get outta my face."

Okay, none of those sounds right.

"Yeah?" Sleepy voice.

"Karissa?"

"Yeah?"

Shoot, I woke her up. And she's not that far along in her pregnancy, which means she probably needs more sleep than usual. Maybe I should have thought more about timing here. Should I just hang up and call again?

"Hello?" she says. "Who is this?"

"Karissa, it's Scotty Dawn, Seth's friend."

"Oh."

"Yeah. He said I should call you."

She sighs. "I can't believe you did. I can't believe you had the guts."

The words aren't said in the Mean Karissa way, more like the Defeated Karissa way.

"Well, he's my good friend."

"Yeah." She grates out a harsh laugh. "You sure ruined it for us."

Okay, this isn't what I called to talk about. "Seth ruined it for you guys. Don't give me credit I don't deserve."

She'll like that.

"You're probably right."

Good, she did.

"I know he told you about what I'm doing. Are you even remotely interested? Because if you aren't, it's okay. It's not going to be a lot of fun, and it's in a small town, a really backward place nothing like Hollywood."

Dad rounds the corner and gives me the thumbs-up/thumbs-down sign. I put my thumb up. He's holding a Coke, too. Good. I'm going to need that thing.

"Can you give me some more info on it?"

"They have a website. What's your e-mail? I'll send it to you."

"Okay. That would be good." She gives me her e-mail. "I'm not even close to making up my mind on this. Seth kinda threw it at me out of the blue."

"He's annoying that way."

She huffs. "You know, Scotty, you don't have to keep throwing your buddy-buddy stuff with Seth in my face, okay?"

"Please, Karissa, Seth and I are like brother and sister—"

"And that too! I hate that stuff. You think you're so much better than everybody else, Scotty, like you're just so smart and you like literature and you write and now you play a stupid harp."

Whoa. So Seth talks about me.

I like it.

Still.

"Look, I'm on my way down to Kentucky. I gotta go."

"Me too."

She clicks off.

Oh brother. Jesus, don't let her come. She'll just ruin what I had hoped would be a really important time in my life.

I slide into the truck.

"How'd that go?" Dad asks, handing me the Coke.

"Pretty much like I expected." I tell him about the conversation.

"You still going to send her the link to the website?"

I pull my laptop out of my knapsack and open it up.

He smiles. "I thought so."

If following Jesus is the right thing to do, why does it make me so mad?

Fifteen minutes later

My cell phone rings.

"Hey, Seth."

"Karissa just called me."

"Was she upset?"

"Yeah."

"Figures."

We're in West Virginia now. Beautiful mountains, scenic views, and I'll bet Dad wishes he'd gotten the V-8 engine instead of the V-6 right now.

"Oh, she wasn't upset at you, Scotty. She was mad at me."

"Why?"

"She wanted to know how I could play savior, seeing as I think I'm too good to be her boyfriend."

"Wow. That sounds pretty intelligent for the Karissa."

"Scotty . . ."

"Sorry."

"So anyway, I doubt she'll be coming down."

Hmm. "So, you two still having lunch?"

"Funny. Very funny."

I hang up. "Well, that's that."

"I gather she's not coming," Dad says as we crest a high hill.

"Nope."

He chuckles. "You know, it's kinda fun having a teenager."

"How so?"

"Think of all the drama I'd miss."

"Funny, Dad. Very funny."

5:30 p.m.

Dad turns between two stone pillars, the one on the right with an oval brass sign engraved with one word: *Meadowgate*.

"Must have been the name of the old farm," Dad says.

The other post bears a sign with the words *Red River Home for Children* in plain block lettering.

Mature trees line the drive. Dad drives the truck into the leafy tunnel, the gravel drive dappled with patches of sunlight. Farther overhead, the mountains shoulder the deep blue of a late-afternoon sky hovering over the summer heat. Farther yet, well, God's looking down. He must be if somehow these kids make it here. I read some of their stories on the Internet. Wow, the human spirit continually amazes me: what we live through, what we'll die for, what we'll give up of ourselves because of love.

The tunnel opens up into a clearing. And there sits the

farmhouse and the activities building. A brightly colored play-ground connects the two. Swing sets for older and younger kids, a rope course, a crazy tall slide, a small slide (there seems to be a big/little theme going on here), and a merry-go-round. Seesaws too. I love seesaws!

"Look! A swimming pool!" I point to the right of the big house.

"Very nice."

Dad pulls into a parking space along the strip of yellow lines perpendicular to the front of the activities center. "Ready?"

I breathe deeply. "Yep. I really am."

Dad puts his hand over mine. "Your mom would have been really proud of you for doing this, for trying to figure out your life in this way, honey."

"Charley said the same thing."

"You could be thinking about what you want your life to mean for you, big career, that sort of thing. Something glam-orous, like a CEO, or acting, I don't know. But you're looking at your life from the perspective of what you can do for others. That's something any parent would be proud of."

"Don't make me a saint, Dad. I may hate it here."

He laughs. "Okay. I'll give you some breathing room."

"I mean, I'm gonna make big mistakes now that I'm putting myself in the position to make them."

"You're right."

"So you're going to have to prepare yourself for that."

"Right."

"Because I'm going to blow it sometimes, Dad."

"Okay! Okay, Scotty, I got it!"

"Just so we're clear." I laugh.

We open the glass double doors and head into the one-story brick building. White letters above the door say The Martha Ehrhardt Building. All the windows make it a bright and sunny place. And did I mention the flowers all around?

Now somebody around here knows such things are important. My ladies at the Design Center would agree.

"It's nice isn't it, Dad?"

The lobby is also a gathering room: comfortable couches and several coffee tables, hardwood floors and thick area rugs, and a stone fireplace for the winter. The bare walls hold shelves and shelves of books.

Books! Gotta love that.

My stomach flips and tumbles as I walk toward the office on the left. Before I can darken the doorway, Megan bursts out looking all cute in jeans, a T-shirt, and bright green Pumas. "You're here! Yay!"

She pulls me into her arms and hugs me close. "I can't believe it! You really came. I am so excited!"

I hug her back. "I know! This is so great!"

Oh, my gosh. I feel so teenagery. So cool.

"This is my dad, Ezra Dawn."

"Pleasure." Dad extends his hand. They shake.

"We'll take good care of her, Mr. Dawn. Although she may love it here so much you'll have to bring her back next summer."

"Gladly." Dad's eyes twinkle.

Her brows knit. "Man you two look alike. No denying her."

"I wouldn't want to."

She sobers. "Around here, those words are heroic."

Wow.

"So come meet the kids! We're setting up for dinner. The

cafeteria's right down the hall." She ushers us down a corridor painted a warm shade of yellow. "It's Thursday, so it's lasagna. Jimmy and Henry in the kitchen make great lasagna. Now they're not so good at stew. Too runny."

I like her.

In the cafeteria, about ten kids set out plates and cutlery.

"What's the age range here?" Dad asks.

"Five through eighteen. We have as many as twenty kids in the residential program. We also have an emergency shelter for kids who are in imminent danger. Sometimes they're as young as several months old. But that's in a special building located just beyond the big house. Hard to see from the drive."

"Wow, quite a ministry." Dad stuffs his hands in his pockets.

"You said it. There's always something crazy going on here. Tomorrow we're taking everyone to the dentist. It'll be a trip! You see that young man over there in the bright green shirt? His name's Alvin. He hates the dentist!"

"How long has he been here?" I ask.

"Two years. We're working with his family so he can go back home, but so far, well, it's not good. You'll see. Each child has his own story. It'll break your heart." She turns to Dad. "Want to stay for dinner?"

He shakes his head. "No thanks. I'm planning on making the drive back home, so I need to get going. Scotty, you going to be okay?"

Panic hits me. I've never been away from an adult in my life! First Charley in the Y, then the TrailMama with Grammie and Grampie, then Dad. What am I doing?

"Dad."

He looks at Megan, who nods. "I've got to help in the kitchen.

I'll leave you two alone."

Dad walks me back to the lobby, sits me on the nearest couch, and takes my hand. "Just say the word, honey, and we'll keep those bags in the truck and go right back home, no questions asked. I won't leave you here unless you're completely comfortable."

What do I do?

I talked all big about learning what it means to act like a Christian. Living the extraordinary life. Trying to be Jesusy. And now here I stand in a place that will help me do just that, and all I want to do is throw myself in the arms of my dad and go away with him.

I remember those beautiful stained-glass windows at Trinity Church in Marshall.

Jesus talking to the scribes in the temple in Jerusalem — going about his Father's business.

Peter walking on the waves.

Be not afraid.

You can do this. I can do this. I'm seventeen years old.

Stop always talking so big, Scotty. Just do it.

Jesus, help me.

Before I can change my mind, I force the words out. "I'll stay."

He nods. "Okay. Let's get your things from the truck."

It's a sloppy, tearful good-bye on my part. And that's all I can say right now.

Leaving my suitcase and backpack in the lobby, I find the bathroom, soak my face in cold water, and cry all over again.

"Hey, what's wrong?"

A girl stands next to me at the sink.

"Sorry, I didn't hear you come in."

"It's okay. I do a lot of crying too. I'm one of those types. My counselor says it's good to get it all out. What's your name?"

"Scotty."

"I'm Belle."

Belle's probably about ten, long-limbed, skinny, with bobbed blond hair, freckles, and an overbite. She's pretty, waifish looking.

"Nice to meet you, Belle."

"I know you just got here. Wanna sit by me at dinner?"

"Thanks. That would be very cool."

By the time we sit down at one of the cafeteria tables, Belle and I are old friends. She plays the violin and likes to bake. "Sometimes"—she sets down her fork—"Henry lets me make hot pretzels, and we eat them while we watch a movie out in the den."

"Do you ever put cheese on the pretzels?"

"Megan makes cheese sauce to dip them in. It's one of our favorite snacks here in the winter."

After dinner, I walk with her back to the big house. She's taken my arm and lays her head against it as we traverse the fine gravel walkway. She talks and talks and talks about her favorite TV show, *The Suite Life of Zack and Cody*, and I don't have a clue as to what she's actually saying, but she thinks it's downright hilarious. And that's definitely enough for me.

7:00 p.m.

The big house is beautiful. They still call it Meadowgate.

While Belle plays with the other kids on the playground (and I saw the little guy Owen with his fire hat), Megan and I climb to the second floor up a wide, carved wooden staircase that's covered with a dark green runner.

"Wow, this was some house in its day, I'll bet."

"Oh yeah. Cool story. This man, MacLellan, came over from Scotland and amassed a fortune in the logging industry, helped build the Nada Tunnel you all drove through. So he built this mansion for the woman he loved back home. They wrote letters all the time, according to the tale, and he finally went back home to marry her." She points to a doorway framed by dark wood. "That's our room. Anyway, when he got there, she'd run off with someone else the week before and eloped."

"That's awful! The poor guy!"

"I know." She lets me go into the room first. "Isn't this pretty? We get the morning sun too."

Two twin beds with lime green comforters hug the wall across from a fireplace with a blue tiled hearth. I point into the cold, scorched recess. "Does it still work?"

"Yes. But we never light it until at least December."

"Oh yeah. I guess it would be too hot."

"It's great here in the winter. Okay, so there's your dresser, and your bed is the one on the right. I need to be near the door because I have to hear when somebody cries out."

"Do you ever get a break?"

"Sure. During the day when the kids are at camp. I do office work after lunch, but I really don't kick in until after they get home. Then I run the tutoring center and supervise dinner and the bedtime ritual. At least with the girls on this floor."

"Where are the boys?"

"Upstairs on the third floor. So back to the story and I'll help you unpack. The closet is right there for your hang-ups."

This sure beats the Rubbermaid tubs in the TrailMama.

"So anyway." She opens my suitcase like she's used to this. Which she is, I guess. "MacLellan turns right back around, comes home, and boards up the house. It sat for twenty years until he signed it over to the home in 1905."

"You've been here that long?"

"Well I haven't." She laughs. "But yeah. We've been doing this for a long, long time."

"That's a lot of kids."

"Yep. Have you ever heard of Raina Masters, the older actress?"

"I love her!"

"She was one of our girls back in the fifties. And Roy Hyde, the senator?"

"Him too?"

"Yes. Pretty amazing isn't it?"

Wow. I didn't realize how far-reaching work like this really is. I'll bet that little Belle will make this place proud someday too. She was playing her violin a little right after dinner.

Brilliant.

I mean it. Really, actually brilliant.

We put away my things, then Megan drags me around for the bedtime ritual, and man is this group a mixed bag. Afterward Megan pulls out a deck of cards from the desk drawer in our room and we play gin rummy.

"Do you have wireless Internet here?" I ask after losing the first hand.

"Yep, over in Ehrhardt."

Very cool.

I'm glad I stayed. Not that I won't cry myself to sleep tonight, but still, Jesus, thanks. And keep Dad safe on the road. I'm still not sure about Babette, and even if she is alive, my father is irreplaceable.

Friday, July 22, 11:00 a.m.

I'm sitting in the cafeteria shelling peas for dinner when Megan runs up. "Let's go! A baby's come up to Hope House."

"Hope House?"

"The emergency housing I told you about."

"Oh, no. A baby? Is it all right?"

"It's a boy. And yes, they got him out just in time. It would have been really bad. I won't go into detail. You're just getting started and some of these things can be overwhelming. But he's safe, so let's go! I love it when we get babies."

"What about the peas?"

"Jimmy!" she yells. "We'll be back in a couple of minutes to finish the peas!"

"No prob!" from the kitchen.

I'm already buds with Jimmy, a squat, redheaded man with broad hands and a big gap between his teeth. He talks about his dogs a lot and lives on the edge of the property in a mobile home with Henry, the other cook, and Crandall, the groundskeeper I haven't met yet, but wow, have I been warned about him! Big advice? Just don't go near the guy. He hates pretty much everybody but a few of the kids. So at least they're okay.

Five minutes later, I'm holding the most beautiful baby I've ever seen. He's only three months old, and his name is Silas. He's asleep. "I'm so glad he's safe," I whisper.

"Me too." Megan runs a tender hand over the downy black hair on Silas's perfect little brown head. "His mother's a drug addict. If the neighbor hadn't called, I don't know what would have become of him. Bad boyfriend on the scene."

"I'm glad he's safe now," I whisper again. "All kids should be safe and loved."

"Well, he'll get plenty of love here. And maybe you were brought here to be the one to do it. Only don't get too attached. He'll probably be sent to foster care in a few days."

"It's probably better for him that way." I sigh.

"It is. And we always find good families. We're picky that way."

"So can I just hold him for the next few days? Can I take care of him, Megan?" I ask it like my life depends on it, and I don't know why the urgency settles in my chest like a steel weight. But somewhere within that mass lies a hope I've never felt before.

She smiles. "Sure. It beats shelling peas is all I know!"

If my mom saw this right now, I know she'd smile.

Fifteen minutes later

While I sit with the sleeping Silas on a blanket behind Hope House, my phone buzzes in my pocket. Text message. I pull it out, trying as hard as I can to not move.

The Karissa? My goodness, as Dad would say.

Karissa: What airport do I fly into?

I quick call Megan on her cell. She picks up and laughs when she realizes it's me.

"Hey," I whisper. "Sorry to call, but I've got a sleeping baby in my arms."

"A girl's gotta do what a girl's gotta do."

"You're right."

"What's up?"

I tell her about the Karissa, her pregnancy, her needs, everything.

"I don't know, Scotty. It's one thing for us to deal with these kids. But a movie star?"

"I know. But isn't she just as precious to God as Silas here?"

I know. Gag me. I can't believe the words come out of my mouth either. Sometimes I wish God were more choosey about who he thinks worthy of a helping hand.

"You're right." She sighs.

"And she is coming as a volunteer, so you can put her to work."

Yeah, right.

"Tell her to come on down. But Scotty, she's going to have to room with us. There are no more free beds."

"Okay. I should have warned you. I seem to collect people. Who knows who else may come?"

"Well, at least I'll know what to expect. You're a trip, girl!"

Yeah, that's me. A veritable trip.

I hit the message button.

Me: Lexington, Kentucky.

Karissa: I'm coming down Monday. Long story.

Wow, she's a full-word texter. I would have *never* pegged her for that.

Me: Can you rent a car? I don't know if there's enough staff to pick you up, and we're about an hour and a half from the airport.

Karissa: Duh.

Me: See you Monday. I'll e-mail you directions from the airport.

Karissa: I'll Google Map it myself. Bye.

Oh. My. Goodness. What have I done?

And did she say she would Google Map it? Maybe there's more to the Karissa than I thought.

Then again, maybe not.

I pull up text messaging on my phone once more.

Me: The Karissa is coming Monday.

Seth: Wow. u ok w it?

Me: Gotta be. What did you tell her?

Seth: I promsd id do all i cn 2 gt hr into my 1st flm nxt yr. scorsese again.

Me: She's not even coming down because she thinks she needs it?!!

Seth: I dnt care hw she gts out of Hollywood. sh jst nds 2 gt out.

Me: But still. It's going to make my job a whole lot more difficult.

Seth: Srry. bt if i ddnt thnk u could hndle it i wldnt hve suggstd it.

Me: Nice to know you have so much faith in me. Really. I mean that.

Seth: Ur prtty amazng, sctty.

Oh my gosh! Can you believe this?

Oh right. He's just buttering me up so I won't be mad about Karissa. I can't believe I almost fell for it.

Me: Keep talking, big shot. You may owe me several big ones after the Karissa's visit. You know that, don't you?

Seth: Drat. The flattry ddnt work?

Me: Nope. Not even a little bit.

Seth: Wll, if it means anythng, i do mean it.

Me: Thanks.

We sign off. Is Seth really softening toward me in more than a brotherly way? It sure seems like it, but I'd be crazy to jump to such a conclusion before I'm sure.

And he'd be crazy to fall for an insignificant seventeen-year-old who just so happens to think he hung the moon.

Okay, so maybe he's not so crazy. We all want to be loved, don't we, and loved for who we really are at that?

Saturday, July 23, 7:30 a.m.

I figure I'll read a little before breakfast, so I head with a blanket behind Hope House. I pull out Gatsby for old times' sake and my phone buzzes in my pocket.

"Hi, Mr. Harris. Is everything okay?"

"Aye. As well as can be expected."

"How's Charley?"

"Your grandmother has been quite sick, but this morning she managed to make it downstairs and have some breakfast. Just oatmeal, mind, but still, it was more than the tea and toast she's eaten the past few days."

"That's it? Tea and toast?"

"I'm afraid so."

"She can be a bear when she's sick. Is she treating you all right?"

"Oh"—his voice warms—"she's allowing me to comfort her. We've been mostly sitting outside before a fire in the evenings, much like back at the campground."

"That's good."

I grab a brush and start on my head. The face staring back at me looks tired, but I think I just miss my family. Last night, actually, I slept great. Meadowgate must do that sort of thing for a person.

"Mr. Harris? This is probably a little awkward, but how's the God stuff going? I mean, I know we've talked about this before, and you hinted you wouldn't marry her unless . . ."

"Oh, my dear, yes, I know. And the answer to your question is that she's asked me to pray for her and you and your father. Out loud, mind you, when we're sitting before the fire."

"That's huge."

"Indeed it is."

"Where is she?"

"She's napping. But I thought you'd like an update. And how goes it for you?"

I tell him everything, and he sounds so interested there on the other end. Actually, he *is* interested, because I know acting and Harris only acts when there's a camera rolling.

"Mr. Harris? What if Charley never comes around, never finds God? What will you do then?"

He sighs, and I sit down on my bed, curling my feet beneath me. "I'm in a pickle."

"How so? And why would you break up with her if she doesn't come around?"

"Well, marriage isn't something to be taken lightly, and my faith is the most important thing to me, so entering into marriage with somebody who doesn't share that, well, I'm sure you can see where I'm going."

Hmm. "Then why did you pursue this relationship in the first place? Shouldn't you have thought of this back then?"

"Aye, my dear. But I suppose I was so taken with your grandmother, I wasn't thinking clearly. I haven't been talking with her as though a future is definite. I've been extremely careful, although our hearts probably haven't been."

I grip the phone. "Well, for her sake and yours I hope God yanks her around and gives her all sorts of love she can't deny. Because if that doesn't happen, and you reject her because of your faith, it'll make Jesus look even worse."

"Of course you're exactly right, Scotty."

"I see I should step up my prayers on this."

"Aye, you most certainly should."

"I will then. But you need to keep me posted on all of this, Mr. Harris. You might need some good advice too."

He chuckles. "Such as?"

"Get her involved at that church you've been taking her to.

Let her meet people, let other people love her too. Charley's crying out for a group to belong to. I mean, after all that running we did, right?"

"Point taken. Brilliant, I might add."

We ring off a few minutes later.

So there's that.

And see? He used the word *brilliant*, and it sounded fine.

Sunday, July 24, 10:20 p.m.

Megan and I take a moonlight swim. All the kids are in bed, the older ones reading or doing something quietly until lights out at eleven. Silas sleeps peacefully in his little crib at Hope House, and I swear I carried him around all day today. They have a little Snugli carrier I slung over my shoulder, and how wonderful it was to just look down between the soft folds of the fabric at him in there sleeping. Megan warned me not to get too attached, but clearly my heart didn't heed her words. I'm totally in love.

He's so sweet when he's sucking on his bottles. Silas is my first experience with a baby, and, well, I don't mean to be proud, but I think I'm a natural.

A new teenager arrived today who blew off Belle's welcoming overtures. Jesus, help me, please, because I am *not* a natural with my peer group. But I could have told you that a long time ago.

Megan joins me in the deep end, where I've hooked my lower legs over the side of the pool while the rest of me floats on the water. It always feels good to have your hair spreading out like a mermaid's. "What did you think of the new girl?" I ask.

"Monica? She's okay. She's not as bad as she seems."

"Emo kids drive me crazy. I'll just admit that right up front."

"They drive everybody crazy. It's why they act like that, Scotty. For the attention. But sometimes it gets a little out of hand and they either believe their own press, or, honestly, their life really does suck."

"Sometimes it's hard to tell which is which."

"Oh, totally!" She hooks her legs over the side of the pool too. "But if she's landed here, you can pretty much bet she's the real deal."

Monica looks almost Goth. Dark clothes, pale skin, but not all the creepy makeup and big boots and striped tights and . . . yawn. Come up with something original why don't you? She sat in the corner of the den during evening prayers and snickered every once in a while when "the goodness of the Lord" or "the way you love us, Jesus" was prayed.

"Did you hear her during prayers?" I ask.

"Yep."

"That was kind of disrespectful, don't you think?"

Megan swings her legs back into the pool. "Uh, Scotty?"

I swing mine back in and we hold onto the ledge. "Yeah?"

"You'll do a whole lot better to view Monica as Jesus might. He can handle her disrespect. But he obviously brought her here to be loved. You can either be part of that or not. Your choice."

Whoa.

She continues. "I'd suggest you be a part, otherwise being here is going to be a bust for you. It's easy to love babies like Silas. I mean, who wouldn't, right?"

"Except for his mom?"

"Okay, I mean around here. We're all crazy about kids. Loving somebody like Monica is where it really gets hard. But succeeding at anything hard is also the most rewarding."

She's right. "How long will she be here?"

"I don't know. I don't see her home situation working out anytime soon."

"What happened?"

"She attacked her stepdad. He raped her on a regular basis. Monica's mom thinks she's making it all up, so she sent her here claiming Monica is completely out of hand."

"Oh, wow."

"Yeah. Things are usually different than they seem."

That sure is the truth.

Thirty minutes later

I climb into bed, all showered and with my hair in pink foam rollers. Gonna be cute tomorrow! Especially with the Karissa coming. She should get here around four. Crandall, the grounds-keeper and, I also found out, general handyman and keeper of anything that doesn't move, brought up a third bed from storage. With some extra linens from the closet and a pink comforter it's not too bad. I'm sure it's nothing like she's used to, though.

Crandall is the most crotchety old guy I've ever met! I like him. He actually irons his overalls. I mean, what is that? I tried to talk, and he brushed me off with rusty grunts. I'm going to get through to him in the next few weeks if it's the last thing I do.

I'm nervous about tomorrow. Isn't that just silly? Please! Karissa Bonano? I must be slipping in my old age.

But I'm tired. After a busy weekend taking care of Silas, helping with yard work, scrubbing the kitchen with Henry and Jimmy, ushering everyone over to the Methodist church down the street for Sunday service, letting Belle paint my fingernails ten times at least, and organizing a game of dodge ball even though I've never played dodge ball in my life and have only seen the movie as reference, well, I'm worn out I guess.

I wouldn't want to be anyplace else, though. I can tell you that.

Monday, July 25, 10:00 a.m.

Megan ushers me into the director's office. Ms. Cook had been away at a conference, but she seems fresh and ready for bear. (Whatever that means.) All I can tell you is the woman looks like she runs the place. Which she does.

"Scotty! Good to meet you."

She should so be selling things for a living. I'd buy pretty much anything from someone with green eyes that twinkle like hers, and hair as red as Karissa's eyes after a night on the town. Two bright patches of blush sit on full cheeks and azalea-pink lips smile at me. She wears a lavender polyester skirt and a floral blouse with buttons slightly straining at her bosom.

And her fingernails! Definitely nail tips, bright pink, little dewdrop diamonds on her pinkies and thumbs.

"Nice to meet you, Ms. Cook."

"We're real glad to have you here. You enjoying Kentucky so far?"

"I really am."

Megan steps forward. "We're taking some of the kids hiking up Natural Bridge today. The older ones."

"Good for you. And what's this I hear about Karissa Bonano coming?"

My jaw drops. "You've heard of her? No way!"

"Sure have. My younger daughter thinks she's great. Now I've heard a thing or two about the young woman . . ."

Megan fills her in on the situation.

She crosses her arms and stares at her employee. "You sure you want to deal with this right now?"

"I think we'll be fine." She turns to me. "Right, Scotty?"

The question is all bright and cheery.

Uh, I wouldn't be so sure about that, Megan. "Right! We'll be fine. And we'll do our best to stay out of your hair."

"Good. I've got to tell you, it's going to be a very busy week for me. The less on my plate the better."

"You got it!" Megan pulls me from the room, and we say our good-byes as we exit. She squeezes my arm out in the hallway. "What are we going to do if Karissa turns out to be a nightmare? How much time are we going to give her?" she asks.

"As long as you say, Megan. Personally, I'll have no trouble telling her to take a hike if we need to."

"Good." Megan sighs in relief. "Because I'm not going to take any of that petty Hollywood starlet stuff like you see on TV."

Oh, man. Karissa's going to last two, three days tops.

11:40 a.m.

Heading over to Ehrhardt, I stop by Crandall, who's planting bulbs outside the playground fence.

"Crocuses?" I ask.

He sits back on his heels and visors his eyes with a flattened hand. "Yes, they are. How'd you know?"

I crouch down and pick up one of the brown, papery bulbs between finger and thumb. "I don't know. I guess I've always liked them. What else are you planting?"

"Asters. Mums. Black-eyed Susans. Coneflowers. Somethin' for every season."

"That's a great idea. Your flowers are beautiful, Mr. Crandall."

"They'd better be. I work hard enough at them!"

I laugh.

He turns back around to his work.

"Henry's chili for lunch," I say.

He grunts.

Lunchtime

So I set my tray with chili, tater tots (baked to just the right golden crispiness, I might add), and fresh-fruit cup on the cafeteria table. Right next to Monica.

She looks up at me and scowls.

I scoot onto the seat and pick up my spoon. Okay, so I have

absolutely no idea what to say right now. I could go a few directions. For one, I could complain about the food and act like we're all buddy-buddy. But Henry and Jimmy are good cooks. Even this girl would see through that. Besides—I look at her plate—she's eaten every bite.

For two, I could talk about how yummy, yummy, yummy it all is and two, four, six, eight, cafeteria food is really great! Goooooo, Henry!

Like, that's so me.

For three, I could just say hi and leave it at that. Let her warm up to me, but let her know I'm around.

"Hi," I say.

She scowls again.

"No prob," I say, then put away the food like I haven't eaten in three days. I'm eating in a cafeteria! It's kinda like being at high school or something, only I imagine this food is much better. Monica just sits tapping her fingernails on the table and looking out the window.

"Okay." I ball up my napkin and throw it on my tray. "Have a great day. I'll see you later."

It's pretty much the best I can do. And it's a start. Right?

4:20 p.m.

Silas and I lounge on a blanket near the playground while the other kids run around a bit before dinner. He's a smiley little guy and pretty alert for a three-month-old. Mrs. Lowe, one of the ladies who runs Hope House, showed me how to give him a bath earlier today. He peed all over me and we laughed. Oh those little hands and feet and the feel of them all soapy and wet made me think of my mother and what she must have felt like when she bathed me.

This is a gift right now. It's like I'm getting to experience my own babyhood through Silas. I feel closer to Mom than I ever have before for some reason. Dead or alive, it doesn't matter.

It's warm out today. A slight breeze rolls over us, thank goodness, through the hardwoods of the eastern Kentucky mountains. I lie down beside Silas and close my eyes against the sunshine.

So peaceful.

Coming here is one of the best things I've ever done.

I feel a tap on my shoulder and open my eyes. "Hi, Belle."

"Hey, Miss Scotty. You all taking a nap?"

"Just dozing a little. There's more blanket if you want to join us."

"Well, all right, I guess I will." She bares her crooked teeth in a wide smile as she lies down on the other side of the baby. "He's a nice little fella, ain't he? I like him."

"Me too."

"Can I hold him?"

"Sure."

I settle him into her arms, and the urge to pray hits me, and I go with it because it doesn't happen very often, unless I'm praying about my own stuff. *Jesus, let her be a good mother someday. Don't let whatever Belle has been through pass down through her to yet another generation. Would you do this, please?*

A red convertible pulls into the parking strip. Its driver wears a scarf and sunglasses, both of which she peels off before disembarking.

The Karissa.

And another thing, Jesus? Would you let me not be a jerk? Would you let me see Karissa like I see Belle, and Silas, and even Monica, even though she hasn't said boo to me?

"Karissa!" I holler and wave.

She turns toward me. "I'll be right back, Belle." I scoop Silas up into my arms and hurry over.

Oh, man. She's dressed so Hollywood. Skin-tight everything, a short skirt, loads of makeup, glitzy jewelry. And that car. Well, I guess she thinks getting a good word in to Scorsese is worth it.

"How was your trip?" I ask. I'm going to kill her with kindness. If it's true that God brought her here, like he did Monica and Belle, Silas, and even me, I'm not going to be the one who sends her packing. But man, is this going to be painful. I'm just sayin'.

"Long. I need a shower and some peace and quiet. Where's my room?"

"You're sharing a room with me and Megan."

"What?" She hikes her Louis Vuitton bag onto her shoulder. "Nobody said anything about sharing a room."

"You didn't ask, did you?" Oh, shoot. "But it's okay!" I brighten my tone. "Megan and I are out all the time except for the evening. You'll have time to yourself." *If you decide not to lift a finger and help these poor kids, that is.*

She lets out a breezy, dramatic sigh and oh, poor thing. Like, I'm feeling *so* sorry for her.

Don't forget about her baby, Scotty. There are two people standing in front of you and the one hasn't done a thing to deserve your attitude.

"Let me help you with your stuff."

"Oh, all right."

Whatever. Or something.

She opens the trunk, three large suitcases stuffed inside.

"Whoa," I say. It just slips out.

"What?"

"Nothing. Let's get some help. Wanna come to the office with me?"

"I'll wait here. I've got to make a couple of calls."

I rearrange Silas to my other arm's crook. "The signal here is terrible. The only place you can make a call is back behind Hope House."

"Great." She rolls her eyes.

You said it, honey.

I think about a part of the Gospels where Jesus says if you think about murdering someone, it's just the same as if you do it. So if you want to slap someone silly, I guess it stands to reason that's the same as doing it too. Man. Jesus didn't mince words is all I can say!

"Hang on. I'll get Crandall."

As I walk away, she mutters, "I can hardly wait."

I whip around. "Would you like to carry them all yourself?" Calm down, Scotty. "Karissa, as you can see" — I hold up Silas — "there are a lot of people here in need of help. This isn't a hotel, and it's not a place where people will serve you. If Crandall helps you, it's because he's a giving person not because you're impressing him."

"Whatever."

Oh, sheesh. I turn back around and head toward Crandall's shed. Good, he's there, repairing an end table from the den.

"We have somebody coming to stay, and she has way too much luggage. Can you help us?"

He puffs out an aggravated breath between his lips. "What's her deal? Can't carry her own weight?"

"Pretty much. I'm sorry."

He looks at Silas and smiles. "Ain't he cute? Love them little ones. Aww, all right. Point the way, honey."

See? I told you he wasn't so bad.

Karissa's still trying her cell phone when we arrive at the car.

Crandall rubs a hand over his short gray hair. "That thing's not going to work here. Gotta go—"

"I know! Over behind the Hope House. Wherever that is."

Crandall turns to me and raises his brows. "Then why you tryin' it here if you know better?"

She glares at him.

"You know, missy, they say the definition of insanity is to try the same thing over and over in hopes of a different outcome. You insane or somethin'?"

"No, I just . . ." She stops, mouth still open.

Karissa has met her match!

I am so loving this.

Sorry, Jesus. But I am.

"Now where're them bags I been hearing about?"

"In the trunk?" she says.

"Well is they or ain't they?"

"Yes, they're in there."

"Let me get 'em, then. Goodness, young women are so empty-headed these days!"

Karissa stares at me, and I just shrug.

She grabs a rolling bag, I take the carry-on, Crandall hefts a suitcase the size of Tom Cruise's ego, and we walk up the path to Meadowgate.

The nice thing? Crandall's saying everything I'm thinking. I don't have to utter one word.

4:45 p.m.

Looking remarkably like Monica, Karissa scowls at the bed as she unzips her large suitcase. Louis Vuitton again. Good grief. "There are really no other rooms?"

"Nope."

"Who's the baby?"

"Silas. Came a couple days ago. Foster parents will take him soon. Drug addict for a mother."

She *pffs*. "I know what *that's* like. Poor kid."

I could jump on that, in a good way, but something tells me to keep silent about it.

"He's a good baby. Want to see?"

"Sure. Why not?"

I draw closer and raise him a little. "Doesn't he have the bluest eyes?"

"Yeah. And with that brown skin."

"He hardly ever cries."

Her mouth hardens. "Probably didn't do any good at home."

Oh. That's true. "You're right."

She sighs. Dramatically. "I really need that shower."

"Okay." I take her to the doorway and point down the hall.

"Third door on your right. And the hot water heater's not all that great, so you'd better be quick."

"Figures."

"Dinner's at six tonight in Ehrhardt, the building you parked in front of."

"I'm not hungry."

Of course you're not.

"There's nothing good in town. Just a greasy place called Tropical Treat. It's neither tropical nor a treat from what I hear."

"I said I'm not hungry."

"But . . ." the baby?

"Don't you listen, you little nitwit?"

My anger flares. "I'm not the one pregnant and drinking, Karissa!"

"He *told* you!"

Oh, shoot.

"Gotta go! Silas should be back at Hope House in a couple of minutes."

And believe me, I beat it out of there!

After dropping Silas off to Mrs. Lowe, who wears bright blue stretch pants and a cotton smock and almost-purple hair (I want to kiss her she's so sweet!) I head to the spot behind the house where the cell signal is clear.

So . . . fiveish here means ten or elevenish in Scotland.

I call Charley.

"Hey, baby." Her voice is sleepy. Darn.

"I didn't mean to wake you up."

"It's okay."

"Is Harris there?"

Silence. "Uh . . . you're kidding, right?"

"Just checking to make sure he's being the gentleman he promised he'd be."

"Perfectly sweet and respectful."

"You sound like you're feeling better. A little anyway."

A wail erupts from over at the playground. Hope it isn't serious.

"I just needed some time and some of Anthony's chicken soup." She clears her throat. "I'm kind of wondering if he really wants me around though. I mean, the relationship isn't progressing like I thought."

"What do you mean?"

"Well, I thought he'd say he loves me by this time and maybe even kiss me. I know he feels things, but . . . I don't know."

"Maybe he just needs companionship. You do like each other, and you have a lot in common, right?"

"It's true. And it sure beats being alone. And it wasn't like Jeremy was beating down my door."

"True. So, you were talking about that church. How's that been going?"

"Well! I met some ladies that have a sewing circle and they're showing me some beautiful ways to embroider. And knit! My knitting is coming a long way. I'm making you a Christmas present right now."

Oh, Charley. "I love you so much."

"I love you too, baby. So much. How are *you* doing? I wasn't much help during our last call."

"I'm okay." I sit down cross-legged in grass Crandall mowed yesterday. "So many cool things are coming my way." I tell her about the children's home, Silas especially, even the Karissa. She laughs at that.

"You must be doing good if you see her as a good thing!"

"I know! She's as obnoxious as ever too. It's pretty bad, and she only got here forty minutes ago."

"Oh, baby. In spite of Karissa, you're being blessed. Harris talks about his blessings all the time, and he talks about my blessings all the time. I'm wondering if I've been focusing on the wrong things all my life."

"What do you mean?"

"All the negative stuff. I mean, I know I tried to act all happy and light and all" — yeah right! — "but I've always focused primarily on what I don't have, or what I thought I wasn't getting. And always looking for the solutions in the wrong places."

"How's Harris any different? Isn't he just another man?"

She breathes in and whispers, "Now there's where you're wrong, baby. He's the type of guy I should have waited for all along."

"Wow."

"Yeah. He's such a believer, if you know what I mean."

"No, not really."

"He's got all this faith. Like he knows God's going to work things out, even through all those years of loneliness after his wife died. And he really loved her, baby. Like, *really* really. And he still went on, and he didn't blame God for it all. He's amazing."

Maybe she'll want some of that for herself. "That's so cool, Charley. Hang on to that guy."

"You mean that?"

"I really do."

"Well let's hope he'll feel the same way."

We exchange a few more words, then, because I know she's

tired, I tell her I have to go. Connection to Scotland discon-
nected for now.

I call Seth.

"Hey, Scotty."

"Karissa didn't know I knew she was pregnant?!"

"Hello, Seth. Nice to hear your voice. I miss you. I'm all lonely
down here in Kentucky with no friends—"

"Okay, I get it. I get it." I sigh. "So?"

"Is she mad at me?"

"You bet she is!"

He laughs. "Good. I don't want her to develop more feelings. I'd rather her be mad than think I'm her knight in shining
armor."

"You said it. She got here forty-five minutes ago and has
already complained a dozen times. This is going to be a long
couple of weeks."

"You can handle it, Scotty. If anybody can, you can."

"Thanks. I'll remember that when I want to slap her silly."

"And if you need me to come down, I will."

"No thanks! You need to stay as far away from that girl as
possible."

A shadow falls across me.

Monica?

"Gotta go. See ya." And I punch the off button. "Hey,
Monica."

"Hi."

"What brings you over here?"

"Just walking around."

I hold up my phone. "I was just making a call."

"Chuh—yeah . . ."

Oh brother. "To my grandmother. She raised me."

Monica throws herself on the grass. "Big deal. Want a medal for that? My grandmother raised me too."

"Oh yeah?"

"Yeah. No big deal."

"So why are you here?"

"I had to go back with my mom and my stepdad. He's a creep."

"I'm sorry."

"Hey, I'm still here."

"Wearing all that black."

She turns to me. "It's pretty much all I've got, so deal with it."

"I will."

"That little baby you're always walking around with is nice, though. Poor kid doesn't have a chance in this world."

"Hopefully some good foster parents will take him in. He deserves it."

"They all do! Every little baby."

"Well, yeah. Of course."

She hops back up. That was quick. "I'd like to hold him tomorrow if that's okay."

"Sure."

"You, like, his nanny around here?"

"During the day." I nod.

"Cool." And she walks off without another word.

My goodness, as Dad would say.

It's amazing what a little baby will do.

I think about you, Jesus. You were a little baby once, and you changed the world.

Tuesday, July 26, 10:00 a.m.

Silas is taking his morning nap, so I'm heading over to the pool for a quick swim before helping Henry and Jimmy in the kitchen. With my black tank swimsuit and a pair of black running shorts, well, I guess I'm going all Monica at the pool. I grab a towel and my heavy-duty sunscreen and that's it.

Quiet hovers over the grounds this morning, except for Crandall's trimmer buzzing somewhere down by the road. An artist from Lexington came in to do projects with the kids over in Ehrhardt. I saw her earlier wearing black and hot pink, her dark hair pulled up into a sloppy French twist, her small feet in black platform sandals. Those kids are going to have a ball.

I open the gate in the fence surrounding the pool.

Oh my goodness.

She's already here, iPod earbuds in her ear canals and a bikini that would fit a toddler if said toddler's mother wanted her to look like a woman fishing for compliments from the wrong kind of guy. Karissa's got a beautiful tan, I'll give her that. Golden and glowing and natural. Guess she got tired of the Hollywood spray-on junk. White gold bangles circle one slender wrist. Darn it, I have to admit it, she's pretty.

But the Red River Home for Children is not the place for this sort of getup. Honestly, I don't know what she's thinking. Is she that oblivious to her whereabouts, to the people she's found herself with?

I guess the answer to that would be yes.

Anyway.

I throw my towel onto the lounger next to hers and start slathering on the sunscreen.

She opens her eyes. "Oh. Hey."

"Hi, Karissa. Great tan. Really."

"Thanks." She closes her eyes again.

Covered with goo, I jump into the pool. Doing laps will be good. I mean, I'd planned on just floating around, but with Karissa taking up all that emotional space and looking all "I don't care what these nice people think or if this place has standards different from my own," I don't want to be framed with guilt by association. She's on her own with that attitude. And that outfit, or lack thereof, as well.

I'm not a good swimmer. Breast stroke all the way, baby, and it feels good, the water rushing gently past me as I slice through it, the sun warming my wet curls. Nice.

This is a great way to think and talk to Jesus, who's had to listen to a whole lot more of my rigmarole lately. Good thing he can hear it all and love me anyway. I wonder if he gets tired of it?

A voice cuts through the peace.

" . . . not the sort of place for that . . . attire. Or lack of it."

See?

Ms. Cook. Not in lavender today, but dusty rose. She sits down in my chair, right on my towel. No prob.

Karissa sits up and huffs at her.

Ms. Cook gentles her voice. "Look, honey, this is a children's home, not the Beverly Hills Hotel. You just can't dress like this. And I'm not sure what your expectations were, but unless you're one of the children sent our way, well, we expect you to carry your weight."

"*Work?*"

"Yes. It'll be good for you."

Karissa sits up. "I *do* know how to work hard. I am an actress, you know."

"Oh, yes. I know. My granddaughter loves your movies. Especially when you were young. That one where you and your sister found yourselves in Hawaii without your parents is her favorite."

Karissa looks like she would yawn if she could get away with it.

"Honey, go change. Look at Scotty over there."

Oh, great.

"Wear something like that, and we'll get along just fine. What's the rest of your wardrobe like? More of the trollop look?"

I slam my hand over my mouth to keep the giant guffaw from erupting. I'll bet Karissa doesn't even know what *trollop* means!

Karissa jams her towel and iPod and moisturizer and lip balm and only the Lord knows what else into her bag and exits the pool on four inch slides.

Ms. Cook turns to me. "Now Scotty, it isn't that I blame you for inviting her here, but we will ask her to leave if her attitude doesn't shape up. We just don't have time for this."

"I understand." I haul myself out of the pool. "I don't blame you. I don't know why I opened my big mouth."

"Obviously she needs to get away from the West Coast. But was there a specific reason you asked her here?"

"She's pregnant, Ms. Cook. And a mutual friend of ours is scared for her because she's been drinking too much."

"Ah. Well, we'll see what we can do. It may take a miracle. But then"—she winks—"we see a lot of those here."

"So there's hope." Frankly, I can't imagine it.

"Oh, honey. There's always hope."

Fifteen minutes later

Ugh. I have to go into our room, and, believe me, I think I'd rather be caught picking my nose in front of the president right now. But this is my room and Megan's, and I'm not going to let her take it over like she did my coffee shop in Marshall. I'm just sayin'.

Best tactic? Look busy.

I rush in, throw my stuff on the bed and start rifling through my dresser for clothes.

"I guess you thought that little exchange at the pool was hilarious," she says.

"Not really." I keep digging, kneeling by the bottom drawer. "I'm outta here."

"Suit yourself."

She slides off her bed and over to my dresser. She crosses her arms over her stomach, and she's still wearing that blasted bathing suit. "Of course, you'll have to admit to Seth that you failed in this little endeavor."

I sit back on my heels. Whoa, not a good view of that suit from here. I jump to my feet. "You're kidding me, right?"

"No. You only want to save me so that he thinks you're so great."

I look up at the ceiling. Jesus, you're going to have to help me big time. "You know, Karissa, in a way you're right. But my failure won't make Seth care about me any less. It's not like that with us."

"Yeah, right."

I shrug. "I'm not going there. Sorry."

"What's the matter with you? You used to come back at me a lot more than you do now. You're so fake now."

"Maybe. Or maybe I'm trying to give you the benefit of the doubt."

Okay, Jesus, that was a big fat lie. I'm sorry. I said it nicely but felt all smarmy inside.

Megan walks in. "Hey, ladies."

"Hi, Megan." I scrape my clean clothes off the dresser. "I'm heading to shower and then to the kitchen. Henry got a load of tomatoes in and we're going to can them today. See ya!"

As I head out the door, Megan says, "Karissa, we need to talk."

I stop in the hallway, just beyond their sight but well within hearing. Growing up around movie sets, I can eavesdrop with the best of them.

"I already heard the scoop from the old lady," Karissa says.

"First of all, that old lady's name is Ms. Cook. Last year, she basically rescued ten children from terrible abuse. And that was only last year. She's been doing this for thirty years, so I think she might deserve a little more respect from you than that."

Nothing from Karissa.

Bedsprings creak as somebody sits down.

"Look, Karissa, none of us really wanted you to come here except for Scotty, and she couldn't give me a good explanation other than you've gotten yourself in a little trouble."

"Hmpf."

"How old are you?"

"Twenty."

"I'm twenty-four so not much difference. Here's the deal. This is totally your decision. You can stay here and try to figure things out, help out a little, maybe get to know some of the kids. I've done a little research on you, and I know you didn't have it easy as a kid yourself."

More silence.

"Am I right?"

"Yeah. But that's all water under the bridge now."

"Even if we divorce our parents, some of that water sticks to us no matter how we long for it to dry up."

She divorced her parents? How did I not know this?

"What do you know about it?"

"Not much personally. I've got a really great family. But I've seen enough of it here, heard stories that would probably make you cringe."

A part of me wants to know some of those stories, but another part me knows I'd never be the same if I did.

Nothing from Karissa.

The bedsprings squeak again and Megan's voice sounds a little closer as she says, "I'll give you two days to decide. In the meantime, try and stay relatively clothed."

I run down the hallway and slide into the shower room, slam into the shower stall, and whip the curtain closed.

Whew.

"I know you were listening, Scotty." Megan laughs.

But I don't say a word!

A few minutes later, when I emerge from the shower wrapped up in my towel, who should I find sitting on the counter but Belle, cradling her violin.

"Scotty! Wanna hear my new song?"

"Sure. It'll sound great in here with all this tile."

She hops down, all gangly and sweet, but my goodness, when

she puts that instrument under her chin and straightens her posture, a graceful arm readying the bow to hover over the strings, she looks queenly, so graceful and full of loveliness I almost catch my breath. This sweet little thing!

And she starts in, playing a jazzy, skippy little number that sounds like something from the twenties or thirties. The phrasing isn't a straight one-two, but filled with syncopation. The notes rise clear and strong to bounce across the room and back again, and her skinny body sways with the rhythm as she smiles, her eyes closed.

When she finishes, drawing off the final stroke to end in a resounding note, I clap my hands as best I can while trying to hold up my towel. "Bravo! Bravo! That was absolutely wonderful! You're amazing!"

Then I pull her to me with my free arm and give her the fullest hug I can. "You're a remarkable little girl, Belle."

She gets shy. New for Belle. "Thanks."

"What was that song?"

"'Exactly Like You.'"

"I love it."

"You do?" Her light gray eyes widen. "Really?"

"You're gonna go far with that instrument, Belle. Keep at it."

"Oh I will!"

She runs out of the shower room, and I hear the song echoing in the hallway as she leaves the floor.

Yes, Jesus. It's times like these, isn't it? This is what all this is about, isn't it? Simple moments, extraordinary times.

6:45 p.m.

My hands are prunes. I peeled a crate of tomatoes this afternoon and was more than ready for dinner. Fried chicken, mashed potatoes, and green beans. Peach pie for dessert.

I'm sitting out on the lawn with Silas. He's getting sleepy, and bedtime is coming soon for the little guy.

Megan pulled Karissa aside, probably to put a little salve on the gaping wound she thinks she inflicted earlier (yeah, right!), and they're sitting on one of the benches lining the walkway from Ehrhardt to the parking strip.

I reach down and pat Silas's little belly, and he grins. "Hey, guy . . ." I croon, and his smile stretches across his toothless, pink gums. I swear he knows me now.

Near Karissa, the bushes rustle, and it isn't the wind. Huh? A lens pops through the foliage. I can't believe this! A photographer!

"Hey!" I stand up.

Karissa and Megan look over at me.

"Right there!" I point toward the bushes. "Paparazzi!"

"Oh no way!" Karissa jumps to her feet and rushes him. "Get out of here! You scum! Get out of here!"

The guy takes off, his legs pumping like steam engines as he runs across the lawn.

Wow.

I walk over with Silas in my arms. "I can't believe it."

Karissa sits calmly back down on the bench and crosses one leg over the other. "I hate those guys so much."

"How did they find you?" Megan asks.

Karissa just shrugs.

9:50 p.m.

I head out behind Hope House to wait for Dad's call. Sure enough, ten o'clock on the dot, my phone rings.

"Dad!"

"Honey! How's it going?"

"Great! What are you doing?"

"Just finishing up work for the day. Grampie made a big salad for dinner, and I'm starving. I'm about to go make a sandwich before heading to bed."

I tell him about the food here. Again. He's had to hear about it every time he calls.

"Hey, I've got something I want to run by you."

"Shoot."

"I'm trying to figure out what we're going to do once you get back."

"What do you mean?"

"I put my notice in with the FBI. I just don't want to put myself at any risk now. I don't have much hope for finding your mom anymore, honey. I haven't heard a thing from Vince, and he was my last lead. I won't leave you all alone. Of course, you'd have your grandparents, but they're just not the same."

"No. Not really. I mean I love them, but . . ."

"So now that Vince has my contact info, we may have to get brand-new identities. Be thinking about what name you'd like."

"Frances."

"Well, that was quick!"

"Hey, I don't mess around."

I look around me to make sure nobody has ventured into the clearing. "Do you think Vince will come after us? Or get the mob after us?"

"I doubt it. My guess: Vince just wants to disappear again. So anyway be thinking about where you want to live. Make up a list of your five top spots."

"Will do."

Wednesday, July 27, 7:00 a.m.

Ms. Cook storms into our bedroom, red in the face and wearing peach.

She pokes a sleeping Karissa, who swats her away, mutters a foul expletive, and rolls over in the bed. Ms. Cook pokes her again. "Wake up. Right now."

Oh my gosh.

Karissa sits up.

"What was that photographer doing here last night?"

"I don't know. I have no idea."

"Who knows you're here?"

"Just Seth. And, well, I think I told a few other people."

Ms. Cook settled her hands on her hips. "Do you have any idea what you've done?"

Karissa just stares at her, mouth open.

"You don't even realize it, do you? That man, taking pictures of you, was also taking pictures of all the kids in the background. Some of them come from very volatile situations. Some of them are here so their parents won't find them. And that picture would have gone all over the Internet."

Karissa's eyes widen. "I didn't think . . ."

"No. You didn't think. This isn't Hollywood, Miss Bonano. This is real life, and these kids have been through enough pain. But it's their pain, and it has nothing to do with your life and your image. Now did you or did you not leak your whereabouts?"

Karissa slips into actress mode, playing the part of the innocent teenager vying for pity. "I swear, Ms. Cook, I didn't tell anybody I didn't think I could trust."

"You actually trust people out there? Oh, honey, you do have a lot to learn. Well, that guy won't be coming back."

"What happened?" I ask.

"Crandall got to him at the end of the drive and smashed his memory stick right out of his camera."

"Good!" I say.

She turns back to Karissa. "Miss Bonano, you have one day left. You either figure out how you can stay here without making all these waves, or you'll have to leave." She storms out.

I sit down on the end of my bed. "Karissa?"

"What?"

"I've got an idea."

"I'm sure it's fabulous."

"Hire somebody to sit down at the end of the drive as a lookout and a deterrent."

"Why would I go through all that trouble?" She reaches over to the nightstand for her lip balm.

"Because maybe, underneath who you project yourself to be, there's somebody who'll do what's decent. You're supposed to be here. The fact that you ended up at this children's home at all is proof of that. So the question is, are you going to waste an opportunity that might give you some clearer understanding, or are you going to go back to LA and be exactly who you were before? I'm heading down to breakfast."

7:45 a.m.

Biscuits and gravy. And I'm talkin' homemade biscuits with crispy, golden bottom crusts. Amazing. Sausage patties and home fries too. I load on the gravy and, okay, yes, I think I've gained a few pounds, but honestly, food like this doesn't come along much in a girl's life. I don't know how Megan doesn't look like a porker.

I slide in next to her. "How come you don't gain weight here?"

"Oh, you get used to it after a while. You just haven't been through Henry and Jimmy's repertoire a good eight hundred and fifty times like I have."

About half the amount of food I have sits on her plate. Oh, well! I'm not going to be here forever. I jab my fork into the sausage, slice off a piece and swirl it in the white, peppery gravy, and into my mouth it goes. Jesus, you do give us good things, don't you?

Call me silly, but I've decided not to be like Charley was for all those years, focusing on the negatives and what I don't have. Right now, I have a really good breakfast. I'm fine with that.

"Can I sit here?"

I glance up and to my left. Monica. "Sure. Have a seat."

She starts gobbling up her food as soon as her butt hits the bench. I've never seen anybody eat so fast.

"You like the food here?"

"It's food. I like to eat food."

Come to think of it, under all that black drapery, she's bone thin. I can come up with multiple scenarios as to why this is, and none of them is pretty. Unless, of course, she just has a high metabolism. I mean it could just be that simple, right?

In three minutes, her breakfast is gone. She even scraped up the remaining bits of gravy with a quarter of a biscuit. I like her style.

I sip my coffee. "So what are you all doing today?" I ask her.

"Service day. The main classroom needs to be painted, and I have asthma so I don't deal well with the fumes. Megan said to make myself busy with the younger kids, so I was wondering if I could come up to Hope House with you and help take care of Silas."

Call me crazy, but I just wasn't expecting this from Monica.

"Do you have any brothers and sisters?"

She shakes her head. "Just me."

"I'm an only child too. Sure, why not? As soon as I'm done we'll head up there."

We've had this entire conversation, and she's yet to crack a smile. Well, if anybody can change that, it'll be little Silas.

8:30 a.m.

Silas wiggles his arms and legs, happy and excited when I walk into the crib room. He's the only infant here right now, and I suspect he's been awake for a little while. There's not much sleepiness around his eyes and his grin.

I curl my fingers underneath his arms, slide them around his tiny back, and lift him from the crib. "He holds his head up really well, doesn't he?"

Monica nods.

She stands close as I warm up his bottle, and we both sit in rocking chairs in the parlor. It isn't long before I notice she keeps the back and forth of her chair in perfect time with mine. Silas sucks away at a bottle with bright yellow daisies all over it. "We won't tell him he's drinking out of a girl bottle," I say.

I cast a furtive glance at Monica, and yes! One side of her mouth is lifted in a half smile.

I will *so* take it!

She shadows me after the feeding, all the way through the bath, diapering, and dressing him in a green Onesie undershirt and a pair of blue socks. "Let's take him outside."

"I guess fresh air must be good for babies."

"I think you're right."

We head down toward the playground. I like it there. Belle always comes by and some of the other kids do too. Josh and Jake, twin boys, always trying to one-up each other in a crazy form of kung-fu gymnastics, can get me laughing harder than a donkey. Owen's swinging, fire hat still perched on his head. "Hey, Miss Scotty!" he yells.

"Hey, Mr. Fireman!"

He laughs and laughs.

I spread out a soft, worn quilt, big enough for the three of us and probably a few more, too.

Monica sits down. "Can I hold him a little bit?"

"Sure."

It's obvious she doesn't know much about holding babies, but then a few days ago, neither did I. Still, she picks it up quickly, and soon he's settled in the crook of her arm, his little behind resting on her lap.

"Hey."

Oh. Karissa. Whoa. "Hi. What's up?"

"Can I sit down?"

"Sure."

And here everything was going so well.

But Karissa looks like she's trying. She's wearing jeans and a pink T and flip-flops. No makeup. Hair in a ponytail. She looks sixteen. Honestly, I don't think I've ever seen her look lovely before. But she does today, more like the little girls she used to play in films when she was young. I haven't seen that Karissa in a long time.

She lies down on the blanket beside Monica. Folds her hands across her stomach and closes her eyes.

I lie down too. "If you want me to hold the baby, just let me know."

The sun warms my face like a light blanket settling down over my features, and I close my eyes in its heat. I think about Dad's call last night. Where will we go after this? I mean, I've got to go to college next year. It's not like this is going to be a simple decision. Five top choices.

Well, DC tops the list. I won't be far from Grammie and

Grampie, Seth, or his parents, Steve and Edie. Great colleges. Exciting area. Next? Oh good grief. I have no idea.

"So why are you here?" Karissa asks Monica.

Okay, I'm not stupid, and I want the scoop. I let out a light snore.

"Stupid mother, her abusive husband. Drink and drugs all day at our . . . hovel. I wasn't going to school much, so my mother said I was out of control. I can't say I wasn't giving her some trouble. I thought she'd kick me out."

No mention of her attack on her stepfather. I don't blame her.

"But she sent you here?"

Belle's voice blasts into the conversation. "Hey y'all! What are you doing?"

"Talking." Karissa says. Interpretation: Go away, you little nuisance.

"Wanna hear me play my song? My violin's right in the center!"

"No. Can't you see we're having a private conversation?"

"Well, I just thought you'd like to—"

"Don't you understand English?" Karissa again. "Leave us alone."

That's it. I sit up. "I'll come hear it, Belle. I love your violin."

I scoop up Silas. "Why don't you two stay here?"

No sense in reprimanding Karissa. Monica's talking to her, don't know why, and that's got to be a good thing. Still, I throw her a daggered glare as I exit. Not that she notices.

Belle takes my free hand as we walk toward Ehrhardt. "My lands, she's a crabby one, ain't she?"

"She's got problems, Belle."

"Still, she don't have to be so mean, does she?"

"No. Just stay away from her."

She holds open the glass door for me and Silas. "But what did I do to her to make her so mad at me?"

We sit down on one of the couches. "Belle, it's like this. There are people in the world who think they're better than some other people. Karissa thinks she's more important than you are."

"Well she ain't."

"No, you're right. Did anybody ever treat you bad in school because they were part of a popular group or something?"

She nods.

"Karissa's like that."

Belle scrunches up her nose. "She's too old to be acting like that."

"You said it."

"Maybe she needs somebody to be really nice to her."

Oh, sheesh. "I don't know if that's it. She's a movie star. People are nice to her all the time."

"But maybe that's be*cause* she's a movie star, and there's a big difference between liking somebody for who they are and liking them because they're important."

Out of the mouths of babes.

"You're right. But I think you're important, and I like you, so play me some more songs, girl! I want to hear every single one you know."

"Really?" She smiles her toothy grin. "You really do?"

"Most definitely."

She runs across the room and plucks her instrument out of her violin case. "You best get comfortable. I know a *lot* of songs."

I do as she suggests, going cross-legged and holding Silas in a sitting-up position so he can see.

Halfway through her first song, a peppy little fiddle number she called "Possum up a Gum Stump," the little guy is mesmerized.

After about eight or so songs, Belle tucks her violin under her arm. "You know, it's nice having somebody listen. Did you know my aunt Sophie taught me to play the fiddle? She was the nicest lady."

"Where did you used to live?"

"Oh, back farther east. My daddy worked in a coal mine. He was in an accident there and died when I was six."

"That's terrible!"

She sits down on the couch next to me. "Then Mother got real sick, and that fast" — she snaps her fingers — "she was dead too."

I settle Silas in one arm and put the other around her. "Were they good parents?"

"Uh-huh. Real good. Our family was small, and my aunt, my daddy's aunt really, she was old and just couldn't take care of me no more. Ms. Cook here is her friend, and so Aunt Sophie brought me here after she sold the home place and then drove herself to a nursing home down the road."

"Do you still get to see her?"

She crosses her legs and sets her fiddle next to her. "Me and Ms. Cook go down once or twice a month. Aunt Sophie can't walk good anymore, but she's still smart as she ever was."

"So you'll stay here until you graduate from high school?"

"Yes. I don't want to go into a foster home. Not with Ms. Cook being so nice. And Henry and Jimmy. Even Crandall's not so bad once you get to know him." She leans forward and whispers, "He gets me a Christmas present, and he doesn't get none of the others one." She grins.

"Well, you're special, Belle. That's plain as day."

"Miss Scotty, can I give you a hug? I think I need one."

And so I draw her close, with Silas in between, lulled to sleep by the little girl's story.

Her blonde hair is clean and sweet, and her shoulder bones stick out, and I love her. *I wish I were old enough to adopt you.* I'd take Silas with me as well.

9:30 p.m.

I just hung up with Dad after giving him my top three places: DC, Asheville, and Memphis. Don't have any other ideas at this point.

I text Seth.

Me: Are you around?

Seth: Yep. Jst finshd shootng and m headed bck 2 th aprtmnt 4 dnnr.

Me: Just you?

Seth: Yes, sctty. sheesh. i'm bhavng myslf.

Me: I wanted to give you a Karissa update.

Seth: Whts hppning?

Me: She almost left today, but I think she's bonded with one of the girls.

Seth: Thts good.

Me: Some paparazzi found her. Director was really miffed. I'm sure it was good for Karissa to realize not everyone in the world is impressed with her.

Seth: Dfinitly.

We text back and forth about my city choices, colleges, and my soon-coming life off the road.

Seth: Wll, i vote 4 dc. well b able 2 c ech othr a lt.

Me: You'd like having your little sis around?

Several minutes pass. Oh. He must have gotten home or had another call come through. Then:

Seth: Who said anythng about lttle sistrs?

Oh my. Oh my. Do I ask him to clarify? What do I do?

Me: Do you have a fever?

Seth: Lol. no. ur jst grwng up sctty. i thnk of u mr lke a friend nw.

Me: Cool. Gotta go. See you later, Seth.

Seth: C ya. B crful.

Just a friend? More than a friend?

And what about Angus? He called me yesterday, all chatty and full of summer news. He's a lifeguard at the country club now, and he had so many funny stories.

Maybe he'll find a girlfriend there!

But, I still kinda like him. I think.

This is totally *not* brilliant.

10:10 p.m.

I stop Megan on my way out of the bathroom, post teeth-brushing. "Can I ask you a question?"

"Sure."

"Is a four-year difference too much for a girl and a guy to date?"

"Whoa, Scotty"—she bobs her eyebrows up and down—"somebody interested in you?"

"I'm not sure. Really not sure. I think maybe. But then I could be reading too much into it."

"Gotcha."

"So? What do you think?"

She leans against the doorjamb. "Seventeen and twenty-one? I don't know. Sounds a bit creepy. Now eighteen and twenty-two. That's a little better."

"That would be like a senior in college dating a freshman."

"It happens." She shrugs.

"Okay. Just checking."

We head into the bedroom. Karissa's painting her toenails.

Megan sits at the end of her bed. "So what did you decide?"

"I'm staying." She looks up through her lashes. "I think maybe I can help Monica out a little bit. We have a lot of the same issues in our lives. They just play out differently."

Megan. "Good."

Karissa shoots a look at me. "And I hired a security company to stay down by the gate. I checked it all out with Ms. Cook, and she seemed satisfied."

I know better than to take credit for this.

"Great! That's really good, Karissa. And I'm glad you and Monica hit it off. I think there's a really neat kid underneath the shroud."

"Maybe I can suggest a makeover?" Karissa.

"No!" both Megan and I yell.

Karissa laughs. "Just kidding. I so got you two."

Wow. Our first ever moment of normal.

11:00 p.m.

Text message comes through.

Dad: Call me right away. News.

I slip into my jeans and flip-flops and run out behind the Hope House.

"What's up?"

"I heard from Vince."

"No way!"

"Yes. He wants to see us in person though. I told him we couldn't get back up there until after you got back."

"Did he say she was dead?"

"No. But Scotty, think about it. If she were alive he would have told me over the phone. You tell good news over the phone, bad news in person. Usually anyway."

"How do you feel?"

"Not much different than before. I know I'd know if she were still alive."

He's just trying to talk himself into the bad news.

I don't blame him.

"So we'll head back up to Maine?"

"You up for it?"

"Oh yeah. Call Helen and Jim and tell them to warm up the campfire."

Okay, then. The search continues. It's all opened up again, and I feel a little hollow searching for a woman I can't remember even one little bit. Just one memory, Jesus. Please.

Thursday, July 28, 2:32 a.m.

Oh my gosh! I sit up in bed.

What if Karissa straightens out her act and Seth goes back to her? I mean, there'd be no good reason not to, right?

Shoot! Shoot, shoot, shoot.

That's it. I have to tell Angus we can't be boyfriend and girlfriend. The truth is, I do care more about Seth, and it's not right to string Angus along. So I take out my notepaper and write a letter. Maybe he'll still come to see me. Maybe he'll realize all he really needed was a friend.

This boy thing is kind of a pain.

And why am I worried about this kind of stuff when I've got my mom to consider, Silas, Karissa and her baby, and famine and disease and pain. This stuff is so heavy.

Oh.

I get it, Jesus.

The silly stuff gets us through the big stuff. It's okay to love and laugh and have fun along with the Jesusy extraordinary stuff too.

I like it.

7:45 p.m.

I don't know if Karissa is playacting, but she and Monica have been chummy all day today. They mopped the cafeteria together, got their fingers messy when Henry decided to show the older kids how to bake bread, and were chatting down at the deep end of the pool during free time. What to make of it? Let's just say I still trust Karissa about as much as a Hollywood lawyer trusts the groom when he's making up a prenup for the bride.

I slip Silas's hands into the armholes of his sleeper—blue with lambies and stars. He yawns.

And he started laughing today! I'd get my face right in his and pull back quickly with a soft little *boo*. He found it downright hilarious. Nobody ever told me that the laugh of an infant is definitely, completely, the absolute best sound in the world.

Now that he's dressed and smelling so good, I sit with him in the crib room's rocking chair, touch the warmed bottle to his lips, and rock him to sleep. I hum a little tune I've always seemed to know.

> *Shine little glowworm, glimmer, glimmer.*
> *Shine little glowworm, glimmer, glimmer.*
> *Lead us lest too far we wander.*
> *Love's sweet voice is callin' yonder.*

I close my eyes, and a memory comes flooding into my brain like a rush of cool water. I see her. I see Babette on her side, lying next to me on my bed, head propped up in her hand. Her dark hair spills over her shoulder, her face pale and smooth and gentle. And she sings softly, her voice a tremory almost-whisper.

She kisses me on both cheeks, then my forehead, my nose, and my lips. "Good night, Baby Boo."

I hold Silas closer to me. Jesus answered my prayer. One memory was all I was asking, and he sent me the best one. I'm sure he did.

My eyes fill with tears, and they spill over my lashes and onto Silas's sleeper. There they'll stay, soaking into the fabric of his dreams. Whatever happens to him, somebody loved him right now. Somebody sang "Glow Worm" to him. Somebody loves him.

Oh, Jesus, if you're inclined to answer one more prayer of mine please answer this one. Protect this baby. Send him to a happy home with good parents. Please, don't ever let him go back to where he came from.

Friday, July 29, 7:30 a.m.

Monica's waiting outside my bedroom door, sitting with her knees to her chest, leaning against the wall. Probably waiting for Karissa to wake up. Hopefully Karissa will be nice to her. It might feel a little disconcerting to have the ghostly shadow that is Monica floating around you all the time.

"Hey, Monica. You're up early."

She slides up the wall to stand. "Could we talk for a minute?"

"Sure. What's up?"

"Can we go to the stairs and sit?"

"Absolutely."

A minute later we sit on the staircase, the middle step. Below us, early morning sun pours through the windows in the upper halves of the front doors.

"So . . ." She rubs her palms on her thighs. "Is Karissa for real?"

Now that's a loaded question!

"What do you mean?"

"She's so nice to me. I mean, it's like we really do have this connection. Here I am growing up poor and weird in Kentucky, and she grew up all cool and glamorous, famous and pretty and all, in Hollywood. And yet we've dealt with all the same problems. It's so weird. I guess, well, I just wonder what's in this for her?"

How astute. And more words than I've heard her say to me in total since she got here.

I sigh. "Monica, has Karissa told you anything about why she came here in the first place?"

She shakes her head.

"It's not my story to tell, but she's got a lot to think about these days and a good reason to do so. Maybe she sees you and doesn't want you to make the same mistakes she has. Maybe she just wants to help."

"It's kinda what I'm hoping."

"I think as long as you don't see her as the key to getting you out of your life, but maybe somebody who's just here, right now, to be understanding, you won't get hurt."

She turns to me. "That's exactly what I'm afraid of. It's so nice to have a friend, Scotty. Like Silas has you. Karissa's kind of like that for me."

"Then just enjoy what you have right now. Most likely, Karissa will have to go back to LA, but she'll still care about you, Monica. She may not be able to wave a magic wand and make all your problems go away, but for right now, it's good having her around. Right?"

She nods. "It'll be hard when she goes, though."

"You're right. But hopefully you'll be stronger than you were before she came."

The strained silence returns. Yeah, I'm not convinced either. Karissa can be a real jerk, but there's always hope, right? I slap my hands on my thighs. "Silas'll be waking up soon."

Monica smiles. "You'd better go get him."

"Okay. You'll be okay?"

"Sure." She shrugs.

"Do I smell?"

"What?"

"I don't think I'll be able to get a shower." I sniff at my armpit.

"You're good."

I head down the steps, get to the bottom and turn around. "Do you know why Karissa's so mean to Belle?"

"She's just annoying, I guess."

Baby steps.

1:30 p.m.

Silas is in for his afternoon nap. Crandall approaches me as I head into Ehrhardt to see what Megan would like me to do.

"Hey there, Scotty." He's holding an orange lawn trimmer.

"Hi, Mr. Crandall. You trimming today?"

"Thinkin' about it. Would be right nice if someone else would do the trimming here by the building so I could go ahead and get the lawn mowed."

I put my hands on my hips. "And you're thinking it might as

well be me?"

"Well, that other prima donna ain't going to, I can tell you that."

"Are you talking about the Karissa?"

"I ain't saying nothing."

I laugh. "Sure. I'll be glad to. Let me have that thing."

He hands it to me. "Now it's gas powered, so it may get a little heavy before long. Just stop and rest a while between muscle spasms." He hacks out a laugh, then shows me how the trimmer works.

"That's loud!"

"Certainly is. Keeps people away from you while you're working. They don't bug you that way."

"I like it."

He heads over to a large riding mower nearby and starts it up. My goodness, we're quite the high-decibel pair!

Crandall takes such good care of this place. I mean, he's not at all good with the kids. Except Belle, I guess. In fact, they're not here long before they learn to give the man his space. But he gifts them with a beautiful place to come heal and learn and be. It's cool how that works, how everybody here brings their piece to the puzzle and how together it makes up a loving picture.

The home's minibus pulls up, and the older elementary- and middle-school-aged kids start stepping out. They went hiking in the gorge and look ready for a snack. "Let's go, gang!" Megan hollers, standing near me and pointing toward the center doors. "Let's get some cool water and some fruit inside you! And then, *chores*!"

They groan.

Karissa comes flying across the lawn, Monica trying to keep

up. Karissa slams into her convertible and throws herself behind the wheel, anger all over her face.

"Karissa!" I yell.

Megan screams as Karissa throws the car in reverse and punches the gas. "Stop! Look behind you!"

"Belle!" I scream.

Belle, a look of terror painting itself on her face, goes down behind Karissa's bumper, her hands outstretched then disappearing, her sunburned cheeks seem to instantly contract to red circles. She screams.

The car halts, a high-pitched screech coming from beneath the wheels.

Oh, Jesus, no!

No! No!

I throw down the trimmer as Megan runs at full speed around the back of Karissa's car. Crandall turns off the mower. Everything stops. The wind. The birds. Everything.

Karissa hops out, and I push past her, throwing her off balance. She bangs her hip into the panel of her car.

Oh, Belle. There she lies.

"Call 9-1-1!" Megan screams.

"Already on the way!" Crandall says, running into the center.

Oh, Belle. Sweet Belle.

Her eyes are closed.

"Move your car forward, Karissa. Now!" Megan yells.

Megan lays her ear against Belle's chest. "Her heart is beating and she's breathing."

"Oh look!" I whisper as Karissa pulls the car forward, moving the tire off of Belle's right hand. "Oh, Jesus." It looks misshapen, the bones clearly broken.

Karissa gets back out of the car. "I'm so sorry."

I turn on her, springing to my feet. "Look what you did! Look at her hand! She plays the violin with that hand, you fool!" I can't help it, something takes over me, and I reach out my hands, connect them with Karissa's shoulders, and push her as hard as I can. She stumbles backward but catches herself. "What's wrong with you? Are you so dissatisfied with ruining your own life you have to ruin someone else's?"

Megan. "Scotty, this isn't helping."

"Get out of here, Karissa. Just get out!"

But Karissa doesn't move. "I'm so sorry. I'm sorry."

"Save it!" I spit out.

"Scotty. Stop it!" Megan. "Come down here with me."

I kneel beside my little friend. Why so much heartache? Oh, Jesus, why *this*?

In the distance, a siren's thin wail begins to thicken, and a minute later, the ambulance appears on the drive.

I watch, praying a jittery, incoherent prayer as they take care of Belle.

"Let's get her to the hospital," one of the paramedics says. "You know who hit her?"

"I did," Karissa says. "I'm so sorry."

"You wait here. The police are on their way."

Megan turns to me. "Call Ms. Cook. Her cell number is taped on the desk in the office. Tell her what happened. I'm heading to the hospital. Ask Crandall to drive you over if you want to come."

"Okay."

She climbs into the back of the ambulance. Everyone is

gathered on the front lawn. Karissa stands by her car, pale and shaking. Monica walks over and stands beside her, saying nothing.

I locate the number, call Ms. Cook, and tell her everything.

"I'm just pulling onto the grounds."

"Can I go to the hospital with you?"

"Be waiting outside, honey."

6:30 p.m.

"She's out of surgery."

Megan whispers the words in my ear, and I sit up. It's amazing how fast sleep can leave a person. But then again, hospital waiting rooms don't usually provide a deep sleep to anybody. We congregate here, wrapped in our worry, and a community somehow develops, each of us linked by fear and love for somebody other than ourselves.

"Is she okay?"

Megan's eyes fill with tears. "The doctor says he's done what he can. Three metacarpals were broken, one in multiple places. Two fingers were broken too."

"Will she be able to play the fiddle again?"

She shakes her head. "I don't know. She'll have to go through a lot of therapy. Age is on her side, though. It's really too soon to tell. Her little chest is bruised, but there was no internal damage, praise the Lord. Karissa wasn't going fast enough, I guess."

"When can we see her?"

"Probably in a couple of hours. But you should go back to the home, Scotty. I'll drive you."

"Okay. Will you come back here?"

"Not tonight. Ms. Cook's going to sit with her this evening and stay the night. Don't worry, we'll have somebody here with her 24/7. You'll get your turn if she's in here long enough."

"Good."

We climb into Ms. Cook's car a few minutes later and head to the home, windows open, a mellow breeze brushing our faces. And it just feels wrong, wrong, wrong to be leaving this hospital.

At least Silas will be waiting. And it'll be bathtime and bottle-time and singtime. He's my little glowworm.

Twenty minutes later

Monica's sitting on one of the benches outside Ehrhardt. "Hey," she says, then stands up.

"Hi, Monica. How's Karissa?" Megan asks.

Wow, Megan's a saint, is all I can say.

"Not good. She's behind Hope House in the garden. She asked me if she could be alone."

"You didn't take that personally I hope." Megan.

She shakes her head. "I've done some bad stuff in my life, but I've never hurt a little kid. I don't think even Karissa would ever dream of doing that."

"I think a lot of her attitude is a cover-up," I say.

"It is."

Megan excuses herself.

I turn to Monica. "I'm going to go talk to her. Where are you going?"

"Inside to watch a movie with the others."

That's good.

"See you later, Monica."

"Yeah."

Crandall's just locking up his shed when I walk by.

"Hey there, Miss Scotty."

"Hi, Crandall."

He asks about Belle, and I give him the news.

"Always have liked that little one. Gots spunk, she does. I'll help her out with that therapy. I know how to do that."

"Really?"

"Uh-huh. It's what I did before the drink got to me and I came here for the peace and quiet."

"That's good, Mr. Crandall."

"Oh, we take care of our own here."

"What happened when the police came?"

"They questioned that actress, well, what they could get out of her anyway, she was crying so hard. It wasn't a hit-and-run or anything, so I don't think there'll be any charges to press. Especially since Belle isn't going to die or nothing. But they said for her to remain in the area a few more days at least."

"She's been arrested before."

"Yeah, they found that out when they radioed her name in. You know I don't like the girl, but I feel sorry for her nonetheless."

"Me too." You know, I do. I really do. "I'm going to head over and talk to her."

"Good luck. I'll say a prayer for you."

"I'm probably the last person she'll want to see." I sigh.

"Then maybe you're the best man for the job."

A few minutes later

Karissa sits on the ground. Dew forms around her, and she is still, legs crossed, hands resting on her knees, head bowed. I approach silently as she sniffs and rubs the palm of her hand up her nose. Bad time to be caught without Kleenex.

I stop beside her. "Hey, Karissa."

She looks up, then back down. "Hi, Scotty."

"Can I sit down?"

She nods.

Okay, Jesus, here's where you come in. I'm not angry at her anymore, and I'm pretty sure it's your doing, so thanks for that. But right now, I need you to tell me the words you want her to hear, because my file of "right things to say" is empty.

We sit in silence for a while, a nightingale singing at the edge of the woods nearby. The crickets scrape out their chirps and the air is still and humid. The day's warmth has only subsided a bit and every breath feels a little like work.

"How is she?" Karissa asks.

"She got out of surgery a little while ago, for her hand."

Karissa gulps. "What . . . ?"

"Several broken bones. It's going to take a lot of therapy for her to get full movement back."

"But she will?"

"They don't know."

She gulps down another sob. "That violin was her ticket out of this place, out of this world."

"Yes," I whisper.

"She was so good. All that talent, right here."

"She plays with her heart."

Karissa starts to weep again. I lay a hand on her shoulder, and she doesn't shrug it off. Waiting for her to speak, I can only guess what she's feeling inside.

Finally. "I'll do whatever it takes to help her get her hand back, Scotty. I swear I will."

"I know, Karissa."

"Yeah, right. Why would you even begin to think that about me?"

"Some things you just know."

"I swear I didn't see her, Scotty. I thought I looked in the rearview mirror. I always look in the mirror."

"Sometimes we just forget to do things when we're upset. What were you so distraught about anyway?"

She shakes her head. "It seems stupid now. I saw some more paparazzi. They got onto the property another way."

"Oh no."

"Normally that wouldn't upset me so much. But I remembered what Ms. Cook said. So I thought if I got away, I'd remove any chance of them taking pictures of the kids. I didn't mean to—" And she erupts in another round of convulsive crying.

I lean forward and wrap both of my arms around her. In a million years, I never would have foreseen this. But my heart is broken for her. She was only trying to do the right thing.

She straightens, and I put my arms back down. "The problem was, even in trying to think about others, I went about it my usual reckless way. Scotty, I'm a screwup. I'm just a mammoth screwup."

"Oh, Karissa . . ."

"You don't have to defend me. In fact, please don't. I have enough people in my life telling me everything I do is fine. You're one of the few who never has."

"I'm sorry."

"No"—she sniffs again—"no, I just don't know what to do now. I just want to leave everything behind. I just want to disappear."

"Sometimes we all do. And that's not always so bad."

"Scotty, I'm sorry. I've been terrible to you, too. You could have been a good friend."

"It's okay, Karissa. I wasn't nice to you either. I've never liked young female stars."

"For good reason."

"It's really okay."

Two minutes later

I think I missed bathtime with Silas, but just in case, I run up the steps inside Hope House to the crib room. Empty. Okay, to the bathroom. Empty. Back to the crib room.

I rush over to his crib.

Oh no!

The mattress is stripped bare.

My hand flies to my mouth.

"He left a few hours ago."

Mrs. Lowe stands in the doorway. She walks over and puts her arm around me. "We found foster parents for him."

The weight of the day's emotions fall on me like a load of wet cement, and I crumble, tears rolling from my eyes. "I didn't realize—"

"No. It happened suddenly. They're a really nice couple. She's an artist who works at home, and he runs a bookstore/coffee shop below where they live."

I grab the railing of the crib. Oh, Silas! "Did you get to meet them?"

"Uh-huh." She nods. "They've been trying to have children for a long time now."

I breathe in a shaky breath. "Do you think they'll get to keep him?"

"I pray so. It's all we can do now."

"Is his mom . . . ?"

"Trying to regain custody?"

I nod.

"Yes. But she's pregnant and—"

"No!"

"Yes."

"Why is it, Mrs. Lowe, that people who would make great parents can't get pregnant and the most awful people keep having children they'll never appreciate?"

She rubs my arm. "Well, Scotty. There's no good answer to that. We can only pray the good Lord sends them to us and to those people who need a baby like Silas to care for."

I wipe my nose.

"Scotty, be happy for him. This is the best we can hope for with babies like Silas."

I turn to her. "Can I meet them? Can I meet these people?"

"I'll call and ask."

Staring down into the empty crib, I run a hand along the plastic-covered mattress. "He is so wonderful."

"One of the sweetest we've ever had here."

"I already miss him so much."

"I know, dear. It's hard. This is what's so hard about life here at the home. We come to love children like our own, but sooner or later, they leave us. Some of them have to go back to their terrible homes. That's even worse."

I believe her, but right now I feel like my heart has been torn from my chest.

10:30 p.m.

Sometimes all we can do is run to God. Because he knows things we don't. To be honest, I'm not angry at him as I lie here, staring at the ceiling of my bedroom. Silas has gone to a good home that God provided for him. God didn't hit Belle with that convertible, Karissa did. I'm really trying to give credit where it's due.

You see, I know from experience that bad things happen on this planet. They have for millennia and they will continue to for as long as we're down here and Jesus is up there. So I can either come to terms with that or fight it with anger and fist-shaking for the rest of my life.

And that will kill me inside.

This is where Jesusy extraordinary fits in, right?

Megan enters the room. "I heard about Silas, Scotty. I'm sorry. This has been a really rough day, hasn't it?"

"Do you have them often?"

"More often than we'd like. But this one was a real doozy."

I sit up as she turns on her bedside lamp. "I'm figuring something out. I think."

"What's that?"

"Well, it's easy to see God working when you're around suffering and the people who need him. But he works by using people like you and Ms. Cook and Crandall. Everybody here."

"It's true."

I throw myself back on my pillow. "So when you make yourself part of the solution, one of the people who give out God's love, you can sort of see he's on it. He still cares about people."

Megan takes off her jewelry. "But some people still slip through the cracks. And that's where it gets hard."

"Why does that happen?"

She sits down on the end of my bed. "Because it's like you say, Scotty, God works through people, and until enough people give a darn, other people will continue to fall through the cracks."

"I hate that."

"Yeah. But it's the way it is. Some people get all mad at God and they never lift a finger to do what he asks them to. But it seems like the people who do the most for others see God in ways they never imagined. I don't understand it. I just see it for what it is."

Karissa enters the room. "I heard what you guys were saying.

You're right." She runs a hand through her hair, pushing it out of her eyes. She looks up at the ceiling. "I've wasted so much of my life."

Megan hops up and leads her over to my bed. "Sit down here with us, Karissa. Now this may all seem a little weird to you both, but Red River is a place where people rely on God to do what they have to do, and so right now, I'm going to pray with you two. If it makes you uncomfortable, just know it's my job." She smiles.

"Go ahead," I say. "I could really use it."

A tear falls down Karissa's cheek. "Nobody's ever prayed with me before."

You did send her here, didn't you, Jesus?

Later, Karissa and Megan sit outside the room long into the night. I don't know what they're saying to each other, but I know God's there too, and Megan's telling Karissa that he loves her. Maybe she's never been told that before. No one told me that for the longest time. And it really is the best news in the world.

Saturday, July 30, 8:00 a.m.

Charley e-mailed me and told me she was going to call this morning. As I sit behind Hope House, the phone rings.

"Charley!"

"Baby!"

She sounds . . . happy!

I could use a dose of that after yesterday.

"You sure sound cheerful."

"I am. Oh, baby! Harris asked me to marry him last night!"

"That's such good news!" In more ways than one, considering Harris's main criteria for who he will marry.

"I know. Are you happy for me, Scotty?"

"Definitely. Are you kidding me? This news is brilliant!"

"I'm so relieved you think so."

"You know how much I like Harris."

"He'll be even more relieved than I am."

"But he's Anthony Harris for heaven's sake."

"Baby, he's so much more than that."

I can see the stars in her eyes from here.

"So when's the wedding?"

She laughs. "At our age, there's no sense in waiting."

"You mean you're getting married over there?"

"Oh no, baby. Not without you! We're coming home in a couple of weeks. I want to get married right on the beach with you and George. Grammie and Grampie too. And I want you to be my maid of honor. Will you?"

"Yes!" I scream. "Yes, yes, yes! Charley, this is the best news. And man, did I need it. I can't wait!"

"Me either."

"But promise me you'll pick out some cool, funky wedding dress over there. And while you're at it, get something just as cool and funky for me to wear too."

"You got it, baby."

Oh my gosh! What did I just do? Charley shopping for me? I think I've lost my mind here.

"Is Harris there?"

"Let me get him."

A minute later. "Hello there, my dear."

"Mr. Harris. Congratulations. Mission accomplished, then?"

"On all fronts."

"How did it happen?"

Harris tells me about a walk in an abbey ruin, the breeze of the religious who once inhabited the halls soaking into them, and how Charley sat down in the middle of the cross of the walls and wept and was filled with faith and hope and love. "And Jesus showed up in the way he does sometimes. We just knew he was there with us."

"Cool."

"Aye, Scotty. Indeed."

9:45 a.m.

"Visiting hours start in fifteen minutes. Wanna go?" I ask.

Karissa jerks her head up. She's planting flowers near Hope House. "Really? Are you sure?"

"Positive."

"But . . ." she holds up a plant.

"I already okayed it with Crandall. I told him I'd help you finish when we came back."

"Thanks! Can I put on clean clothes?"

"Can you hurry?"

She stands up and brushes the dirt from her hands on the legs of her jeans. "Yeah. Scotty, today of all days there's nothing in the world, no cool clothing, makeup, or jewelry that's going to help me do what I've got to do."

"What is that?"

"Ask a little girl for forgiveness."

Ten minutes later we pull off the grounds in her convertible. "Afterwards, do you mind if we go by the rental place for another car?"

"Not at all."

"Maybe we can throw off the paparazzi with that."

"Why aren't they out yet?"

"Because they know I'm never out of bed before noon if I can help it."

"Oh."

"Yeah," she sighs and grips the wheel.

We pull out onto the road.

She taps the steering wheel. "You know, for so long I've been entertaining little girls like Belle. I know some of my old movies are still favorites."

"That's true."

"But it's like I was so young when I did them that I didn't care about the girls who were watching them. And then they've watched me grow up and make a mess of my life. Hitting Belle . . ."

I stay silent, but my head fills in the missing words, *was completely metaphorical for what I've been doing for years.*

Finally, "I know what you're trying to say, Karissa."

"You do? Really?"

"We all have regrets."

"Not like these!"

I smile. "Maybe not. But Belle's a toughie. At least there's that."

She sighs. "I don't know, Scotty. I don't know."

Fifteen minutes later

The children's ward is bright and colorful, with rainbows and flowers and clouds painted on the hallway walls. "Want me to prepare her for you?" I ask Karissa.

"Would you mind? I'd really appreciate it."

"No prob."

I enter the room Belle shares with — I do a quick count — five other children. Yellow walls and ruffled curtains, more murals cheer up the place, and all the kids are watching *SpongeBob SquarePants*. Love that little yellow guy.

Oh, sweet girl. There she sits on her bed, the head raised, her legs Indian style. She seems so skinny and fragile. She spots me.

"Scotty! You came!" She bobs up and down a little, then winces. "Ouch!"

"You gotta be careful."

"I know. I keep forgetting. Look!" She holds up her arm. "A big old cast. And it's itchy!"

"Does it hurt?"

"Well, yeah! But I'm figuring I need to be brave for all the little kids when I go home. They look up to me, you know."

"I sure do." This kid is amazing.

"And they tell me I may not play my fiddle again, but I'm not listening to them doctors, Scotty. I'm going to do all I can to get my hand back in shape."

"Crandall says he used to be a physical therapist."

"I didn't know that." Her eyes go round.

"Me either. He said he'll help you."

She leans forward. "Crandall likes me the best. Now I don't go saying that to the other kids, but it's still just as true."

I whisper, "I know. He told me."

"He did?" She grins.

"Yep. How's your chest?"

"Sore. Wanna see it?"

I laugh. "If you wanna show it."

"Oh I do!" She lifts her gown and oh my goodness. "It's already turning purple, then it'll go black then green then yellow."

"It's true."

"I'll be a rainbow before all's said and done."

"I'm so sorry, Belle."

She shrugs. "It's okay. You didn't do nothing, Scotty."

"What about Karissa? How are you feeling about her?"

"She didn't mean it, did she? They told me it was an accident."

"It was. She feels horrible about it. She's been crying and crying."

"I know I sure would if I hit somebody by accident!"

We laugh together.

"She's outside, Belle. She wants to see you. Would that be all right with you?"

She nods.

I get up and step into the hallway. "Did you hear?"

"Every word. She's amazing, isn't she?"

"Not many like her in the world."

I lead Karissa in, then step to the side as she walks up to the bed. "Hi, Belle."

"Hey, Karissa."

"How are you feeling?"

"Been better, that's for sure!" She grins and wrinkles up her nose.

"Can I sit down?"

"Uh-huh."

Karissa sets her purse on the floor and sits on the bed. "Belle, I am so sorry."

"It's okay."

"No, really. I'm asking for your forgiveness. Please forgive me."

"But it was an accident."

"My brushing you off the past few days and being mean to you wasn't. I'm asking forgiveness for that, too."

"Oh." Belle looks down at her hands. "Miss Karissa, no offense, but people been a lot meaner than that to me. I just wanted to play you one of my songs is all."

Karissa laughs, and her laughter turns to weeping.

Belle holds out her arms. "Oh, come now! You need a big old hug."

And she takes Karissa Bonano, Hollywood's hot young actress, into her embrace. Well, a one-armed embrace anyway.

"And just so you know, I do forgive you."

An hour later

Karissa and I climb into a compact car. It's an old Nissan, dusty gray. The clerk at the rental company looked at her like she'd lost her mind. "You sure you want this old thing, miss?"

"More sure than anyone can possibly realize."

"Suit yourself." He held out the keys.

Karissa snatched them like they were a lifeline.

She starts up the car and turns to me. "I've never had a crappy beater car, Scotty. There's so much about teenage life I missed out on."

"Tell me about it!"

She smiles. "You know, at least we've got that in common."

Truth is, it's probably all we've got in common, but it's enough.

"Do you like eating in the cafeteria at the home?" I ask. "I do."

"I love it! And 'lights out'? Isn't it great? My parents never put any rules on me."

"None?" My mouth drops open. "Even Charley had rules."

"Nope."

"All I know is what I've read in the tabloids over the years."

"Well, that's sort of a skeleton outline. Let's just say a kid doesn't divorce her parents without good reason. I just climbed myself out of the massive financial hole they dug last year."

"Really?"

"Spent it all. Went right up their noses and down the toilet."

"Karissa, I'm really sorry."

"Well, let's just say I didn't deal with it well either."

She turns onto the road leading to the home.

"But you had no guidance."

"I still have a conscience, don't I?"

"Well, if you'd have asked me that a week ago . . ."

"Touché."

Touché? Well, I'll let that one slide.

My cell phone rings. "Hang on a sec."

"Go ahead."

"Hello?"

"Scotty, it's Ms. Cook. Mrs. Lowe told me you wanted to meet Silas's new foster parents. When I told them about you, they said they'd love for you to come over. Want to go right now? I understand you're out with Karissa."

"Definitely!"

"Here's the address and directions."

I dig in my bag for paper and pen and write down the information. "We're on our way."

I explain the situation to Karissa. "Is that okay?"

"Oh, Scotty! I didn't know Silas had left!"

"Yeah."

"Let's go then."

She downshifts and, well, the car doesn't jump forward like she expected.

"Beater cars," I say.

She laughs.

Fifteen minutes later

We drive into Stanton, a small town near the Mountain Parkway. I point toward a brick building with a classy sign swinging over the sidewalk.

"There it is! Oh, how cool!"

They've transformed an old bank building into their home and bookstore/coffee shop. Books and Brew. I like it.

We head inside. The big vault door is opened up behind the

coffee bar. A few mismatched tables are scattered over the wooden floor, and sunlight floods through the tall, arched windows.

Behind the counter, a tall man with ropy black dreadlocks pours beans into a glass jar. Faded jeans and a dark green T-shirt cover his thin frame. He looks up as we approach and smiles like he's known us forever, his dark brown eyes warm and friendly. "Hey there, ladies! How you all doing today?"

"Good," I say. "I'm Scotty Dawn."

"Well, hey!" he says again. "I'm Demetrius Singleton. It's great to meet you!" He comes around the counter. "Ms. Cook called earlier."

"Thanks for letting me come over. This is my friend Karissa."

"Nice to meet you, too!" They shake hands. "Let me go get Sonia."

He runs up a set of stairs to the side.

"He didn't recognize you," I say to Karissa.

"People over thirty-five usually don't. And that's a good thing."

Feet clop down the steps, feet clad in canvas espadrilles. A flouncy linen skirt appears next and then a patchwork tunic, and if all that wasn't enough, a coffee-with-cream face so sweet and clear it should be mandatory for all first-grade teachers. Sonia's auburn hair is pulled onto the very top of her head in a sloppy bun. A paintbrush sticks out of it. Oh, make that two paintbrushes. "Scotty!" she rushes forward, eyes as blue as Silas's smiling into mine. "You're the young lady that took such good care of Silas!"

"I am." I step forward. Because I did. I took good care of that little glowworm.

"He's napping right now." She hugs me tight. "We're so

thankful for you. He's such a wonderful baby, and now we know why."

"Well, he's probably got a lot to do with it."

She laughs. "You're right! Let's have a cup of tea and you can tell me all about him, give me tips, anything you think I might need to know."

"Don't you just love her?" I whisper to Karissa as Sonia makes a pot of tea.

"I'm so happy for that baby, Scotty."

"Me too." And I am. I truly am.

So we sit, our hands curled around fine teacups, and I tell her about how red he gets around the eyes when he's sleepy, that his hungry cry sounds like little pantings, and his uncomfortable cry, like when he's got too much gas, is a throaty wail. His lonely cry, well, it's a lonely cry, but that doesn't happen too much. Hold him close as much as you can, and he's a happy camper.

I lean forward. "My grandmother told me you can't hold babies too much. That it's a big myth you can spoil them that way."

"I think so too," says Sonia. "I mean, they grow up soon enough and won't want to be held. Someday, you'll yearn for them to sit on your lap, and they'll have more important things to do."

"I'm glad you and Demetrius got him, Sonia. I'll give you another tip. I've been singing 'Glow Worm' to him every night."

"I love that song!" she says.

"Me too." Karissa.

"So you know it?"

"I do. I'll keep up the tradition. It'll be his special song."

"You won't let it go?" I need her to say yes. I need to know that a part of me will stay with my baby for the rest of his life.

"I promise."

I sit back in my chair and smile. Life is good.

Saturday, August 13, 8:45 a.m.

Two weeks later, I pull Monica close. "I am so sorry you have to go back home."

"I don't understand that stupid judge!" Karissa says.

"Me either."

Monica pulls back. "I think I'll be all right this time. It's only two weeks, and then I head to Chicago." She smiles at Karissa.

Karissa got Monica into a private school for the arts. "You'll do great there. I wanted to go there so badly, but I was too busy working."

"With your voice, Monica, you'll do so well."

Okay, so the crazy thing I didn't know about Karissa is that she loves opera. Go figure, right? When she put on one of her CDs (yeah, she was listening to *Aida* on her iPod that day by the pool) Monica sang right along with the soprano. She didn't know the words or anything, but once she knew the melody line, it was, well, transcendent is all I can say. Karissa and I just stared at each other, mouths open.

Belle hopped around us that day. She said, "I'm going to learn the violin part, and you all just see if I don't!"

Karissa hugged her. "I'll do the same for you when the time comes, Belle. You'll practice hard, won't you?"

"I will! I'll get this old hand whipped into shape!"

"Well, don't be too hard on it," I said. "It's too cute."

Her cast is almost covered in signatures.

Monica's mother pulls up. And to describe her would be hateful, because I can't think of a single nice thing to say about her. I really can't.

She just honks the horn. That's it. Doesn't get out of the car to hug her daughter or say so much as boo to her.

Monica's eyes remain dry. Mine do too. But Karissa's tears spill over as the old Duster rolls away.

I put my arm around her shoulders. "You've become a regular crybaby."

"Yeah. It's pretty great. I hadn't cried in a long time before coming here."

"Oh, I find a cry does a girl good every now and then."

I still cry for my little glowworm sometimes. But he's doing great with Sonia and Demetrius. Getting all fat and even happier.

We head to our room and pull out our suitcases. Dad and I are going to drop Karissa off in Lexington and see her onto her flight.

"This was a crazy summer," I say.

"The best one, I think. Despite all the bad things that happened."

I open a dresser drawer. "God does crazy things like that. Makes the bad good somehow."

She sighs. "I think you're right. Scotty, how am I ever going to make it again in LA?"

"A lot of prayer!"

Another sigh. Deeper this time. "It still feels weird to pray.

It's not like you can really act your way into talking to God. Not really. But you know, it's been neat to have someone to talk to who sees me exactly for who I am, no cool getup, no slick lines, no hip friends. Just me."

"It's the best."

"Does God ever talk back?"

"Sometimes. Very special times. You just have to listen close."

"I will."

We continue packing in silence. I hate to leave this place, but there's so much in front of me.

"What will you do, Scotty?"

"Try one more time to find my mom. Then finish up my high school work this year and then next year, college, I guess. We're moving to DC."

"You'd better let me visit you."

"I totally will."

More packing.

Then. "Scotty? I want you to know I won't be pursuing Seth. I've thought a lot about it. I think it's better if we're just friends and leave it at that."

"What makes you say that?"

She reddens.

"Oh. I get it."

"Yeah. I want to turn over a new leaf. And Seth's part of the old leaf. Sometimes it's best to leave behind what we can. He's kinda a reminder of all that. I mean he's a great guy, but . . ."

"I think that's wise."

She sighs. "I don't know what I'm going to do when I get to LA," she says again, tucking a lock of blonde hair behind her ear.

"Well, you could try to find more girls like Monica."

She nods and zips shut suitcase number one. "And get rid of some of these trollop clothes! I mean, what kid wants their mom to be dressed like a tramp?"

"There's a good start." Trollop? She actually used the word *trollop*?

"Let's start right now."

We go through her wardrobe piece by piece. You see, Karissa's a new creation. Megan and Jesus made sure of that before her time here at the home was up.

She rolls her eyes. "I can't believe I ever wore some of this stuff, much less brought it to wear at an *orphanage*!"

"It's hard to see things for what they are in Hollywood."

"Scotty, truer words were never spoken."

I love Karissa. She's my friend.

Miracles can happen.

Wednesday, August 17, 11:15 a.m.

I'm sitting on my rock in Maine, the gentle waves lapping just below my feet. A family in one of the motorboats putters by in search of fish, I suppose. Everyone's orange life vest contrasts with the green of the trees and the gray of the lake. Looks like fun.

Not in the mood for any Hemingway, especially today. My diary, Elaine, is of little use as well.

This is it.

Well, it's a little different here than at the bottom of an empty swimming pool at that campground in Asheville, and I wonder how Angus is doing. He wrote back to say, "Just friends is cool," but cancelled his trip to see me, and he doesn't call anymore. I feel like such a creep, but isn't it better in the long run? Romance hurts. I've still got so much time. I pull out my stationery and start writing more letters. Vince told Dad he'd meet him out here.

Karissa's been texting me like crazy, asking me all sorts of questions, telling me bits of news. I think I'm a sort of lifeline to reality. Here's the thing. I really like her. I just don't think she was really herself before. But deep inside, a nice person was just waiting to be coaxed out.

"Scotty!"

I turn my head. "Hey, Dad!"

"Come on up. We've got a visitor."

I turn further in the chair and look at him. "Is it —"

"Yes. Vince is here."

I go into the TrailMama, fix us all a Coke, then we settle around the picnic table outside. Vince is quiet. He keeps running his hand through his graying brown curls and looking up toward the sky, the light turning his brown eyes to amber. He must have been the looker when he was young.

He's short, with legs like fire hydrants.

"She looks like you did when you were younger," Vince says as Dad slides into his seat.

"So you recognized me."

"Sure. Yeah. You all got those eyes. Can't tattoo over them, can ya?"

"No."

"I always liked you, Georgie. I really did. I was sad when I thought you died."

Dad raises an eyebrow.

He nods. "I mean, yeah, I'd get sad at stuff. I never liked it and all, it was just the way."

I've already decided I'm not saying much here. I'd be stupid if I didn't let Dad do the talking.

He continues. "And yet there's something of her mom around the mouth and the chin. Am I right?"

"You are." Dad.

Then Dad remains silent. His lack of conversation, aimed at propelling Vince forward in his story, starts to work.

"So I'm figuring you're under an alias?" he asks.

"Yes. I can't let the others know I'm not dead. Especially Robertsman."

Vince waves an impatient hand. "That guy. Hated him. A pansy. Letting us do all his dirty work. Although"—he shrugs—"it was a mutually agreeable situation if you know what I mean."

Dad nods.

"And the guy's running for president. Go figure. You think he'll win?"

"Don't know."

"I don't think he will. Even the Mafia can't get a guy into the presidency, although some would beg to differ. I wouldn't worry about him. He's on his own, doing fine. He really thinks you're dead."

But what about the bug in Dad's jacket? You see, we had these warning calls every time Dad, who we thought was trying to harm us, got near to us in his search. Charley and I had been thinking he was sent by Robertsman, who was trying to clean up the last of the smudge marks on his past. I'm not going to ask right now though. Babette was last known to be with this man. He's got a story to tell. We'll work out the details later.

"We all thought you were dead, Georgie."

"Good."

Vince laughs. "Yeah. Good for you. Good for me for disappearing. I still can't believe they haven't found me."

"Peter knows. He gave me the tip."

"Pete? No kiddin'?"

"Yep, Peter gave me the tip."

"And he didn't kill you?"

Dad shakes his head. "He's getting older. Maybe he wants to do some good before it all shakes down for him. I don't know."

"Yeah, maybe. It all catches up sooner or later. No exceptions that I've ever heard."

Dad's dying to ask about Babette. But he's waiting. You can't force these things, I guess.

"So it's safe for me to talk to you," Vince says. "At least right now."

"I think so, Vince."

"Nobody was trailing you?" He sips his Coke.

"No. I'm sure of it."

"Well, I'd trust you as much as anybody on that." He looks at me. "Your father, he was something, young lady." He taps his head. "Smart. A different kind of smart than me. I don't know why I didn't see he was a plant sooner. You can't hide a truly good heart. And your dad has one. Especially if he's been looking for your mother this long."

I nod. "I know." I'm almost scared to speak those words, any words at all for that matter.

Vince looks down. "I wish I had better news to share. You know she was with me?"

"Peter told me she was sick, figured you took her away to care for her," Dad says.

"Yeah. I did. It was like this. She got very weak and tired, and they wouldn't get her to a doctor. I did what I could. They let me take care of her."

"How long was she with you guys?" Dad.

"Three months."

"Why did they keep her around that long?"

"Because of me. I lied. I told them she was my woman."

"Okay." Dad inhales through his nose. "You did what you had to do."

"I did. You had a good woman there, Georgie."

Had. Past tense. Oh, Jesus. No. No. No.

Oh, no.

It all comes upon me. The hope that had been hovering all summer in Kentucky—with each child I held, each tomato I peeled—the hope that laid over me cracks, then crumbles into dust at the base of my heart. "She's dead," I whisper.

"Yeah." Vince's eyes droop. "I tried. I did the best I could."

Dad's face remains like stone. But I know he's dying inside. His hands have curled into fists like he's digging his nails into his palms to keep himself here, in the present. "What was wrong with her? Did she suffer?"

"Yeah. It was leukemia, Georgie. We disappeared one night. Got all my money and I took her out west to a good clinic, but when it became apparent she wasn't gonna make it, we came here for her to die in peace."

"What about us?" I ask. "Did she know about us?"

"I did my best to find you and your grandmother. I sent a friend of mine to ask around the neighborhood, but somebody told her you'd both died in the fire."

I touch Dad's hand. "Charley told her next-door neighbors to say that if anybody asked."

"Didn't she check the death records?" Dad asked.

"No. To be honest, I don't think she wanted to see it in black and white, you know?"

I knew she must have figured we were dead. She'd have moved heaven and earth to find us if she had thought we were alive.

"When did she die?" Dad.

"About two years after the shooting."

Dad looks down at his hands. "It's good to finally know."

"I wish I had better news."

Dad pulls out his bandana and wipes his forehead. "Did you love her?"

Vince hesitates. "I did. But I swear I never did anything that wasn't honorable. She didn't want that even though she thought you were dead, Georgie. She always said she'd love you until the day she died. And she did."

Dad stands. "I think you'd better go now, Vince. For a little while anyway. We have to collect ourselves."

"Yeah, I understand."

"We have a lot more questions. Can we come see you?"

"Sure. I don't think you'll squeal."

"Thanks, Vince," Dad says, holding out his hand, "for taking care of her."

Vince takes Dad's hand, and they shake. "It was an honor."

We watch him slide into his gray sedan, and he drives off, dust puffing out from beneath the wheels.

I turn to my father, and his face breaks into a million pieces. We crumble to our knees together and cry and cry and cry.

Midnight

Dad still sits alone down the shore. I pick up my chair and head back to the RV.

Thursday, August 18, 6:30 a.m.

The world has changed.

A year and a half ago I was complaining about not being able to eat cheese.

I grew up yesterday. I can't explain it any other way. I mean a lot happened in Kentucky too, but this sort of tops it all off. Certain bad news will either make you or break you, as they say.

I make up my bed, throw on shorts and a T-shirt, and set a pan on the stove to heat up. Dad sleeps in Charley's old bedroom cubicle in the back of the RV.

Coffee.

Okay, right. And eggs and toast.

That's it. Nothing more.

My bones are bare. My heart shredded. My tear ducts emptied after crying half the night.

Several minutes later the coffee begins to sputter into the pot and eggs fry in the skillet. I plug in the toaster, set in two slices. They toast while I set the table.

Dad opens his door. He looks horrible. I've never seen him looking so awful. "Bad night."

"Me too."

"I figured."

"Have a seat. The coffee should be ready soon."

He slides onto a dinette bench. "I guess I had more hope than I thought."

"Yeah."

He runs a hand over his thinning hair. "For years I figured she was dead, that I'd know it if she was alive. That feeling kept me going when all the roads seemed to dead-end."

"And then I came along and raised your hopes again. I'm so sorry, Dad."

"Oh, Scotty. That wasn't your fault. I should have known."

"No." I shake my head. "It's human to hope. We have to."

"I guess." He sighs.

I turn back around and pour us each a mug of coffee, then scoop the eggs onto our plates. I set the toast on the side. "I'm sure you're not hungry either, but I thought we should keep up the pretense."

"I agree."

I sit down. "So are we heading back to Vince's today?"

"Sooner the better, I'd say."

"Do you think she's buried near here?"

He nods. "At least we can visit her there."

I take a bite of eggs. Swallow. It's painful. I push my plate to the side. This just isn't going to happen. Dad's actions mimic mine. "Sorry, honey. I appreciate you cooking this, but I just can't."

"You know, I feel so bad she thought we were dead. Man, Dad. It's like her last years were full of grief. I hate that!"

"I do too." He sighs. "If I could just go back to that day. She didn't want me to go in. Did I ever tell you about that?"

"No."

"That morning as I was getting dressed, she told me not to go in. We'd had plans the evening before, we dropped you off at Charley's and went to a dinner, and she begged me to call in sick so we could spend the day together as a family. Go pick you up from your grandmother's, go to the park, anything.

"I laughed it off, telling her that a guy's gotta work, but I could tell she was scared. You know how you feel sometimes when things aren't right?"

"Definitely."

"I think she was feeling that. And I knew what was going down, and I'm sure I wasn't acting my usual self. She had to have picked up on that. What I can't figure out is why I didn't realize she was following me. Do you think she might have thought I was having an affair or something? I've asked myself that over and over again."

"Oh, Dad! No way! You're so not that kind of scumbag."

I piled the full plates. "Let's hurry up and get ready."

He jumps in the shower. I brush my hair—don't care if it's in a style or not today—and sit outside in my pink chair to wait. Jesus, I know I can't expect you to raise my mother from the dead or anything, but maybe you can give my dad and me something to hang on to here. Anything. Any little thing would be better than nothing right now.

Through the window I look deep into the woods at the edge of sight, and something glows. A thin little glimmer. Like a glow-worm. It disappears.

I'll take it.

10:00 a.m.

Dad knocks on Vince's red door.

A few seconds later it opens. "Glad you guys came. Come on in."

He invites us to sit down on a comfy denim sofa and offers us cups of coffee. While he gets the drinks, I admire the room. Spare yet warm, and—my breath catches—on the bookshelf sits a picture of my mother.

"Look, Dad." I point to it.

Dad rises, walks over, and picks it up. He sits back down, and we stare at the picture. She's sitting on the front porch of this very house, extremely thin, a scarf covering her most likely thinned-out hair. She's reading a book, a blanket covering her lower body, obviously not aware the picture is being taken. Even ill, her face is lovely.

Vince walks in. "That was about two months before she died."

"What was she reading?"

"*The Great Gatsby*. It was the last book she read."

My breath catches. Dad grabs my hand. I calm myself. "I like

Fitzgerald too."

"She was a real reader."

"So is Ariana," Dad says.

It feels weird to be called by my real name.

Vince sets cups of coffee on the table in front of us. "I suppose you'll want to know where she's buried?"

"Yes." Dad.

He reaches toward a small writing desk behind him and grabs a sheet of paper. "I drew you up a little map. It's not far from here. A private family cemetery. They said they'd take good care of her."

"Really?" I say.

"Good people, there. And they do take good care of the place. Her grave sits on a—well, you'll see for yourself."

"Thank you." Dad folds up the paper and puts it in his pocket.

"You all have any other questions?"

I sit up. "I do. For a long time we were getting these phone calls, my grandmother and me, warning us when Dad was getting close. Only we didn't know it was Dad, we thought one of Robertsman's guys was after us."

"That guy was you?" Vince turns to my Dad, then takes a seat in a chair opposite the sofa. "Well, that's just the craziest thing."

"What do you mean?" I ask.

"Okay, here's the story. I was at the movies a few years ago. I'm a big Jeremy Winger fan. Saw this kid in one of the scenes, and, Georgie, she was almost a dead ringer for you. Those eyes. Know what I mean?"

"You mentioned that." Dad.

"Yeah. So Babette had mentioned that her mother did food

for pictures and stuff, and I thought, why not? Why not at least try to track this kid down? For Babette's sake."

My mother must have really been something to have instilled such devotion in people. Wow.

"You know," I say, "my grandmother only let me do that sort of thing once. Now I have to wear crazy suits. Like a big bottle of mustard. My grandmother was highly over-protective."

"Good for her." Vince. "So then I started the whole business of finding you. I hired people, you know, the whole deal. They found you a couple of years ago and told me someone was after you."

"They saw me?" Dad.

"Yeah. And I didn't know if you were from Robertsman or the family or what. I couldn't risk going to you guys in person. Not with having fled the organization, so I got somebody to plant that bug on you, Georgie, only I didn't know it was you. And there was one on your scooter, Ariana. I tracked your whereabouts, got your grandmother's phone number through dubious means—"

Dad whistles. "You are good."

"Hey. What can I say? And when he got too close to you, I'd give you guys a call."

"Pretty sophisticated," Dad says.

"Maybe. But I loved Babette, and I was going to protect her child."

"Why didn't you tell me about her?" I ask. "Tell me she was dead?"

He bows his head. "I couldn't. You'd made a life with your grandmother. I just didn't have it in me." He grates out a harsh laugh. "I've broken legs and done my fair share of hurting people, but telling a child her mother is dead was too much

169

even for me."

"Yesterday must have been hard for you," I whisper.

"Yeah. But not as hard as it was for you."

"No. You're right about that."

Dad sets his mug on the coffee table. "That sure answers all of our questions."

"Only Robertsman remains," I say. "And whether we're even on his radar screen anymore, who can say?"

"I think I can find that out," Dad says.

"Good luck with that. He's probably got people a mile thick around him." Vince.

"He should." Dad.

"I really wouldn't worry about him, but the guy is dirtier than a sewer, so maybe you can't be too safe." Vince lays his left ankle on his right knee. "It's good to be outta all that."

"Well, you did a good job keeping yourself hidden," Dad says. "But have you made amends with the people you harmed?"

"I'm working on it, Georgie. Behind the scenes, anonymously. I've confessed it all to my priest and to God. Someday maybe I'll turn myself in. Not yet. I'm considering it though."

"Well, we'll leave you to figure out what your conscience demands. You did right by my wife, though, and I'm thankful. Personally."

He sighs. "She loved you guys. You were lucky to have been loved like that."

I read between the lines: Vince never was.

"Can I ask you for a favor?" I ask.

"Sure, Ariana."

"Do you have anything of my mother's that I could have?"

"Yeah, I do. Hang on."

He disappears down the small hallway and into what I guess is a bedroom. He returns a few seconds later. "Here you go. Take them. I know she would have wanted you to have them. That's for sure."

He hands me a stack of three composition books, the black-and-white speckled covers smooth beneath my fingertips. "She loved writing stories."

"Have you read them?" I ask.

"Yeah. She was working on a story. She never finished it. But it was almost done."

"What about her journal?" Dad.

"She told me to burn it when she died. I did."

Oh, Jesus! Not that!

"Thank you, Vince," Dad says. He turns to me. "We'd better go. I think we have a grave site to visit."

"And one more thing." He turns to the bookshelf and pulls a paperback from between the stacks. "Take this too."

I catch my breath. My mother's copy of *The Great Gatsby*. I hold it to my heart, then up to my nose, breathing in the scent of the paper and maybe even a little bit of her, too.

I flip the pages and the smell of roses, her perfume, rises into the air. I inhale it as far down into my lungs as it will go.

11:00 a.m.

We enter the small cemetery on top of a high hill behind Pittston Farm. The walk up the steep incline has left us a little winded, so we stop just inside the waist-high wrought-iron fence.

"It's beautiful here."

Trees surround us, the graveyard itself opening up a patch of sky as blue as my father's eyes. I breathe deeply.

"It is," Dad says. "She would have approved."

"I'm sure Vince showed it to her. Don't you think?"

"I do."

He pulls the map out of his shirt pocket, opens it up, and points to the small diagram of the cemetery Vince drew out. "She's straight back from here in the back row." Then he laughs.

"What's funny?"

"Her favorite spot at press conferences."

I smile. "That's cool. I mean, she's gone, so at least she's in a spot she'd find comfortable."

"She picked it. I can feel it."

He steps forward and so do I, tucking my hand in his. Trees surround the small cemetery, their summer green hovering around the edges of our journey.

It's funny how life takes these turns. It can become so serious in a flash, and we're left doing the things we've always done, like walking and breathing. And we'll walk up to her grave and there will be leaves on the ground and the sun overhead. And we'll stand there, just looking down.

This is exactly what happens.

At the top of the grave, a chiseled granite headstone bears the words "Babette Wethington, loving wife and mother."

"He didn't say friend," Dad says. "Vince left himself out even though he took care of her."

"I know."

Dad kneels down and runs a tender hand over the grass where

I guess her head would be. "Oh, darlin'. I'm so sorry."

I stay put. So much of his relationship with her has nothing to do with me. Let him be with that part of her. I sit down at the foot of the grave and run my hand over the grass above her feet. Oh, Mom.

She didn't deserve to end up here. Not so young anyway.

I bow my head and let the sun soak into my hair and shoulders. The breeze caresses my neck, and I just sit with her because this is all I have of her, all I ever will have, and I'll take it. Because I have to. That is all.

Thirty minutes later

"Ariana?"

I look up. Dad still sits in his spot. "Yeah, Dad?"

"Come on over."

I scramble to my feet and sit on his Indian-style lap. He hugs me, and I lean back against him. We look out over the valley below us.

He clears his throat. "I want you to know I'm sorry for this."

"What do you mean?"

"I guess it's my fault she's here. My chosen profession led to this, didn't it?"

I crane my neck back to look at him. I'm so glad I've already decided how *this* conversation should go. "Dad, no! Of course not. She died from leukemia. She would have died had none of the rest happened. You heard what Vince said. He took her to the best doctors. You can't blame yourself."

"But she died without us."

"You did what you thought was right. You did what *was* right. Mom had to have known she was taking that chance when she married you, didn't she?"

"Yes. She was quite brave about it too. Very aware. But she didn't know how far in I was. She thought I was just a step above a computer geek."

"Like you are now."

He laughs. "Yes. Like I am now."

"You *are* a computer geek now, right? And for someone other than the FBI? Because I don't know if I'm going to be so brave as she was. Promise?"

"I promise. I'm not going to do anything to jeopardize what we have. Never again."

"I'll hold you to it," I say.

"I hope you will."

"Dad, Mom wasn't stupid. You know she knew the truth about what you did. Maybe not the particulars, but I'll bet she knew."

"Maybe you're right, honey."

I pull out the notebook containing the beginning of her story and begin to read aloud. "'There was once a little girl who lived on Long Island. She spent half her summers reading *The Great Gatsby* in a large oak tree overlooking the sound. She loved to read about the fancy parties and the women who wore jeweled dresses. She could almost hear the music of the orchestra and the pounding of fine leather and satin shoes as they danced the Charleston. She was very poor.'"

An hour later, I break in the reading. "I just feel like I can't leave her, can't go away from here."

"Me too, honey. But we have to. We can't stay here forever."

"Can we come back tomorrow?"

"Yes. We'll come back tomorrow."

Friday, August 19, 12:20 p.m.

Dad pulls up in front of Vince's. We get out of the truck and knock on the door. No answer.

"He must be pulling his hermit trick again," I say.

Dad looks into the living room window and shakes his head. "No. I wouldn't say that's the case today."

"Why?" I step toward the window.

"Look inside."

I peer in. The furniture sits just as it did yesterday. But the framed snapshots are gone, the afghan from the couch, and a shelf full of books. "He's gone."

"Yes, honey."

"But why?"

"He knew what I'd have to do."

I look at Dad, his mouth in a grim line. "I don't understand."

"Honey, I'll have to turn him in."

"Oh, Dad!"

"He knew that."

"But didn't you say you appreciated what he did for Mom?"

"Personally."

"So he knew what you were talking about?"

"Yes. He got it. Or he wouldn't be gone today."

I sit on one of the porch chairs. "Wow. He just gave up his life for us. So we'd know."

Dad sits down too. "Yes, he did. And he did it for your mother, too."

I think about that. "Of course. Of course he did."

Poor Vince. Life, good and bad, mercy and justice, aren't always easy, are they?

Twenty minutes later

I tell Babette all about it as Dad fishes in his pickup truck for the spade we bought at the hardware store. "He was a good man to you, I know. I know he's a criminal, but there's a part of me that hopes he gets away. But I don't blame Dad!" I reassure her and myself.

From my pants pocket I slide out a copy of her picture that I made last night. I already feel connected to her. I always have been. She was and is my mother. Even death doesn't cut that off. Maybe I don't remember her, but she carried me in her womb, birthed me on June 6 seventeen years ago, carried me home from the hospital, changed my diapers, fed me, rocked me to sleep. She helped me take my first steps, potty trained me, took me for walks in the stroller, and swung me at the park. I'll bet she read me little cardboard books and played patty-cake.

She sang "Glow Worm" to me.

She told me she loved me, and she kissed me over and over again like mothers do. She blew raspberries into the soft folds of my neck. And I laughed, and one day she dropped me off at my grandmother's and never came back. What did I think? Did I wait and wait, wondering each day until I realized this new lady was taking care of me? And what day did I forget her completely and assume Charley was my mother? No wonder she always had me call her Charley.

Dad's shadow falls across the grave in front of me. "Ready to leave a part of us behind with her?"

"Definitely."

"Let's get the rest of the flowers."

We lift a flat of perennials out of the back of the pickup truck, some black-eyed Susans, two coneflower plants, asters, and a mess of crocus and daffodil bulbs for the spring. Thank you, Crandall. Dad thought I was a veritable greenhouse of knowledge at the nursery.

He sets down his share of the plants. "It will be the prettiest grave anybody's ever seen."

We kneel on the turf and Dad thrusts the spade into the rich ground, the soil dark and moist when overturned. I place the plants and together we pat them firmly into earth that was spooned over my mother's coffin almost a decade and a half ago.

I lean back, sitting on my heels. "Do you think she sees? Like maybe God's letting her take a peek?"

"I'm not sure how it works, but I'd like to think that maybe sometimes she does."

"Only the good times, though."

I mean, really, I'd hate for her to see me when I'm yelling at Seth or visiting those foul Hollywood gossip sites. I'd hate her to see me tearing people down like I'm prone to do.

"Ready?" Dad says. "We've got an early start tomorrow."

"Just a few more minutes?"

"Okay, honey. A few more."

Monday, August 22, 9:10 a.m.

My cell phone rings.

"Charley!"

"Baby!"

"How's it going?"

"Good. I don't know why I missed all of your messages and your dad's. It must be the time difference, and we're out in the middle of nowhere most of the time. We're in Dumfries right now. We just finished up dinner at Hullabaloo. Are you still in Maine?"

"We got home from Maine two days ago."

"Oh yeah?"

She's hoping for good news. I can hear it in her voice. The little upswing on the end of *yeah*, the breathy tone.

"Charley?"

"Yeah, baby."

"Are you sitting down?"

"I'm in the car with Anthony."

"I didn't want to tell you this in a voice mail."

Silence. Then, "Oh no."

I see her so clearly. She closes her beautiful eyes and leans her head back against the car's headrest.

"Charley, Mom died two years after she disappeared."

"What happened?" Tears fill her voice, barely a whisper.

"It was leukemia." And I tell her the entirety of the tale. She asks questions, barely able to talk, but somehow gets the words out.

When I tell her about Vince she says, "I'm glad she had somebody to take care of her. At least she had that."

And I tell her about the beautiful grave site and the flowers that we planted, how we didn't want to leave.

"I'll go there too," she says. "Oh, Babette."

And she breaks down, finally, in a fit of weeping so full and throaty that I cry too, right here on the beach.

The phone clatters down. She dropped it. I hear her say, "Babette's gone. She's buried in Maine. My baby's dead."

A second later. "Scotty, it's Harris."

"Mr. Harris." I throw back my grief. "I'm sorry I had to tell her over the phone."

"You had no choice but to, my dear."

"Will she be all right?"

"I'll take it from here. I love your grandmother very much. She'll get the best of care."

"Thank you. I wish we could all be together right now."

"We'll fly back so you and she can go up to Maine together."

"Will you come too?" I ask.

"Aye, if you'd like."

And in this moment, I realize Anthony Harris is a part of the family. I tell him, "You're family now. You have to come."

His own voice thickens as he says, "Thank you, Scotty. I'll most certainly be there. It will be an honor."

Saturday, September 3, 7:30 p.m.

The evening breeze rolls in off the ocean, and a poppy red sun warms the skies over the bay.

Charley takes Harris's hands. Her blue eyes rest in his gaze, and love fills that gaze. I don't think I've ever seen two people so loved by each other.

"Oh, Dad," I whisper. "Were you and Mom like that?"

"Yes. Just as silly in love as that pair."

"I like it," I whisper. "So much I can't stand it."

We assemble on the sand, the surf every once in a while tickling our bare feet. Charley's gauzy, pale-yellow dress, its hem uneven and otherworldly, swings around her ankles. My dress, a blush pink, and from a vintage shop in Glasgow (I am just sayin'!) brushes its lace and long sash against my calves. We set wreaths of fresh flowers on our heads.

Harris looks brilliant in his kilt, and Dad, who's standing up for him, shines in one as well. My goodness, we're just a stunning family tonight! Sorry, but if you can't think a little highly of yourself and the people you love on a wedding day, when can you?

They speak their vows, Harris promising in the tried-and-true words of "love and honor, sickness and health, until death do us part," and Charley, bless her hippie heart, rambles on about lifetimes of love and two hearts meeting and beating as one, and, well, what can I say? She's my grandmother, and I love her.

The minister pronounces them husband and wife, and Angus, who agreed he and I were destined to be good friends, pipes a joyful Celtic song and the two dance something ancient yet new, something joyful yet solemn.

Harris raises up his arms and says, "Rejoice with us. Any dance'll do!"

Dad puts his hand out. "Shall we?"

I settle mine in his. "Naturally."

Grampie settles Grammie in the circle of his arms for a mean little fox trot, Jeremy and Miss Burrell do a two-step, and Dad and I waltz. And waltz and waltz.

The sun sets in a deep-pink sky as we celebrate life and love and family.

Thank you, Jesus. You went above and beyond the call of duty this time. Grace covers us, fills us, and lifts us up. It's a wedding day. And it just doesn't get better than this.

Sunday, September 4, 3:20 p.m.

Dad, my dad, my cool dad (and yes, I'm still in awe I get to have a dad), slides a key into the lock of our new apartment on K Street in downtown DC.

When we pulled up to the brick building, I squealed. A real city apartment building. And it's not old and gross either.

I'm still on a high from the wedding. Charley and Harris left yesterday for a honeymoon in the tropics. Harris wouldn't tell anybody where because it was a surprise for his new bride, and how cute is that?

"Now it isn't really fancy, Scotty." Dad turns the knob. "Just walls and beige carpet, a galley kitchen—"

"What's that?"

"A small kitchen."

"Smaller than the RV?"

"Well no . . ."

"So there you go! Come on, Dad, open the door!"

He pushes it open, and there it is, our place. Me and Dad. Here in the nation's capital. Among colleges and jobs and a whole new life. A new identity for both of us.

I rush forward into the empty room. And start laughing. "Dad, we have no furniture. Just our clothes and personal things."

"Isn't it great?" He gets down on the carpet and starts rolling around the empty room.

I follow suit. Our laughter echoes off the bare walls and windows. We laugh until our sides ache.

"Oh, Dad." I sit up and catch my breath. "What possessed you to do that?"

"Your mom and I used to do this every time we moved to a new place, before our stuff came."

I inch next to him, and he puts an arm around my shoulders. We just sit, staring around us.

"Wanna see the bedrooms and the bath?"

"Yeah!" I hop up.

I follow him down the hallway to the room at the end.

"So this is obviously yours," I say. "The master bedroom."

He ushers me inside. "Nope. It's yours."

"No way, Dad. I'm so not going to let you do that."

"Scotty. I'm an old guy. I've had lots of bedrooms in my time."

"I've got one at Grammie's."

"It's not the same. All I need is a bed, a dresser, and my desk. Look at me! I'm not exactly Mr. Metro."

I cross my arms. "I dunno, Dad. You smelled pretty nice when you came to pick me up in Kentucky."

"You have clothes and well, girl stuff. Just all that stuff."

"Brilliant!" I throw my arms around his neck. "Thanks, Dad!"

"Now we can't paint or anything, but I have no doubt you'll make this place your own."

"Most definitely."

"Then tomorrow we'll do a little shopping for some furniture. How does that sound?"

"Very, very cool. We've got to find some thrift stores though, Dad. Find the cool stuff. And it's cheaper too!"

"You got it. Let's go get some coffee."

But I sit down right in the middle of my floor. "Can you get it carryout and bring it back home?"

And does it ever feel good to say that.

"Will do."

"Dad? What are we named now?"

Dad has established that Robertsman, the creep, isn't on our tails. But we can't be too careful concerning the mob. So Dad's giving himself a new look. His hair is short now, and he's ditched the biker clothes. Dockers and easy button-downs cover his tattoos. You know, he's still a looker! Can't seem to lose weight, though, much to his chagrin. But I can't imagine him skinny. I really can't.

"Well, they thought the Scotty Fitzgerald thing was a little over the top, no offense to Charley. But they don't think it'll hurt to keep it. So Scotty Fitzgerald Dawn it still is."

"You still going with Ezra?"

"I never made that official. What do you think?"

"I don't know, Dad. It never suited you. How about just going with a relative's name? How about . . . Do you have a grandfather you liked?"

"His name was Art."

"Art? I love it! It sounds so sixties! Like this apartment building."

Dad clears his throat. "I think I'll go get that coffee."

I roll around my bare room. I'm home. I'm finally home. Dad's been transferred to the Department of Agriculture, doing computer work, and I'll finish up homeschool this year in coffee shops and museums and all sorts of cool places in this very cool city.

Watch out, Washington! Scotty Fitzgerald is among your ranks. But she isn't a nobody, as you'll soon find out.

I'm just saying.

Ten months later, June 6, 10:30 p.m.

So I think I keep having "the best day of my life" again and again. I thought meeting Dad was, then Charley's wedding. Now, well, my eighteenth birthday is coming to a close, and I think this was the best day ever because, you see, all the people I love came to celebrate here at Grammie and Grampie's house.

Charley and Harris of course. Still in love and showin' it off!

Ms. Burrell wore leopard print and high heels. Sassy as ever, and, boy, I love that woman.

Jeremy had on his same old hat. Love him too.

Maisie showed up! My RV chatroom friend. And she brought her fiddle, and we danced and clapped and talked about Belle.

Joy Overstreet arrived fashionably late, still fashionable, still plus-sized, and still gorgeous, hottie fiancé in tow. Poor Jeremy. That leathery old guy is destined for consummate bachelorhood. I just can't imagine it any other way.

Steve and Edie Haas arrived early with rumaki and a cheese ball. Edie's been cancer-free for almost ten months now, and how great is that?

Even Jeanne came up from Texas with Grace and little May. May's walking! Life sure whizzes by if you're not paying attention. She brought lots of cards from the gang in Marshall.

Karissa came too. Right now she's helping Grammie and Grampie in the kitchen. True to her word, she's remained friends with Seth, just friends, and put Monica in that arts school. Monica's still a bit of a loner, but no one there can deny that with that voice, she'll do amazing things. "She's even added brown to her wardrobe," Karissa said, and we laughed and laughed.

Karissa looks truly beautiful now. Healthy and, drum roll, a great mom to a little boy she named Luke after her favorite gospel writer. I kid you not. That's what she said. He's asleep on my bed right now. She hasn't filmed since I last saw her but she wrote a book. Wrote. A. Book.

I know, I'm shocked too. The book is all about her conversion. She says most of her old friends turned their backs on her. "It hurt. But sometimes you just have to do what you have to do.

I still love them. They know that, and that I'm here for them if they need me."

I hugged her and told her how proud I am of her.

Megan couldn't come, but she sent a video of the kids at the home, Belle playing "Happy Birthday to You" on her violin, and then she rode to Books and Brew and got some footage of Silas, who's still with Sonia and Demetrius. Adoption papers have been prepared, and he should be officially theirs by the end of summer.

Thank you, Jesus.

And you're here too, aren't you? I think you're smiling at this crazy gathering you've placed around me. A little over two years ago I was so alone.

I miss my mom tonight. But she'd be the first one to say we should be celebrating. So I do, in her honor.

What's taking Dad and Seth so long out on that blasted deck? They both said, "Don't come out!"

And they don't ask much of me, so here I sit in a chair with Mom's *Gatsby* in my lap. Not reading it, mind you. But the old thing comforts me.

Right now, the rest of the crew is down on the beach.

Except for Seth and Dad.

Finally, the sliding door opens. "Honey, Seth wants to talk to you."

"What in the world were you guys discussing out there?" I stand up.

Dad winks. "I think I'll let him tell you."

Karissa looks up from the sink at the bar that divides the kitchen from the family room and grins from ear to ear. "Go, Scotty! Get on out there."

Dad steps aside as I pass through the doors and onto the deck. Although we can't see the ocean from here, I breathe in the salty breeze. "Seth?"

"Scotty. Can we talk?"

I walk over to him. "Are you okay?"

He nods. Then swallows. "I think so. I'm nervous."

"What were you talking to Dad about? Did he give you trouble?" I cross my arms and laugh.

"Yes. Sort of. He had a lot of questions."

"What about?"

"You. And . . . and me, Scotty."

I shake my head. "What are you talking about?"

We walk over to the steps leading down to the yard.

"Sit down," he says. "If you don't mind, that is."

"Wow, you really are nervous."

He sits next to me and takes my hand. "Scotty, I was asking your dad if it was all right if we entered into a relationship."

Oh. My. Gosh. "Like . . . dating?" I whisper.

He nods. "Exactly. Only if you want to I mean!" he rushes on. "I mean, I don't know if you do. I've made so many mistakes. And I haven't always been the friend I should have been. And, Scotty, I'm so sorry."

"Seth, we've been through that. It's over. This past year you've been a great friend. We've had some really good times. And you've come to see us, even when you were busy."

"And I haven't gone out with another soul. I swear."

I smile. "I know."

"So, do you want to go out sometime?" He grins halfway.

"Sure. When?"

"How about right now?"

"And then?" I clear my throat. "It's like this, Seth. I've . . ." How do I say this? Might as well just go on ahead. "I've loved you for so long, and I don't want to get my heart broken. If it's just some dates and all—"

"No, Scotty. I swear it isn't. I love you too."

"Really? Like *love* love, because Seth if you just think you can come along—"

"Scotty, can I kiss you?"

"What?" Did he really just say that?

"Can I?"

I raise one eyebrow. "You really want to? Really?"

He presses his lips to mine. Soft warmth. Then leans back. "Was that okay?"

I nod.

He puts his arms around me and then gently pushes my head onto his shoulder. He lays his cheek against my hair. "I love you, Scotty. And I'll stay around for as long as you'll have me." Raising my face to his, he lays his hands along either side of my face. "So what do you say? Will you let me hang around the place for a while?"

"Hmm. You promise not to be too much of a nuisance? I mean, I'll still want time to read, you know."

He laughs. "You got it."

"And to go to Kentucky every year."

"That's fine."

"And I'm good on the harp now. You may get sick of that."

"Never!"

"And can we get to Graceland at least once a year?"

"You bet."

I lift up my head, cock it to the side. "Well, then, yeah. I guess it'll be okay if we go out."

He kisses me again.

"So, Seth Haas, what's the first thing you want to do?"

"I want to go down to the beach, lie on a blanket, sip coffee from a Thermos and read *The Great Gatsby* by flashlight. How does that sound?"

"I like it."

I really do.

A Thermos and blanket sit at the bottom of the steps. "Ready?" he says.

"Most definitely."

Dad opens the screen door. "You don't want to forget this!" He chucks *Gatsby* at Seth, who catches it.

"Thanks, Mr. Dawn."

"Have her home by midnight. Not a minute later."

"Aye, aye, sir!" He salutes.

Hand in hand we walk to a deserted strip of beach. Though far from the island on which we met, somehow it's the same shore, the same stars, the same moon.

He lays down the blanket, sits on one side. He holds out his hand and pats my spot with other. I join him.

"Ready?" he says, clicking on the flashlight.

"I am."

He opens Mom's book, shines the beam of light on the page, and begins to read. "'In my younger and more vulnerable years my father gave me some advice that I've been turning over in my mind ever since.'

"'Whenever you feel like criticizing anyone,' he told me, 'just remember that all the people in this world haven't had the advantages that you've had.'"

Wow. I am just sayin'.

About the Author

Lisa Samson is the author of twenty books, including the Christy Award-winning *Hollywood Nobody* and *Songbird*. The *Hollywood Nobody* books are her first Young Adult books. She speaks at various writers' conferences throughout the year. Lisa and her husband, Will, reside in Kentucky with their three children. Learn more about Lisa at www.lisasamson.com.

More great titles from the TH1NK fiction line!

Skinny
Laura L. Smith
ISBN-13: 978-1-60006-356-5
ISBN-10: 1-60006-356-X

Melissa Rollins seems to have a perfect life: good grades, good friends, a position on the dance team, and the perfect boyfriend. When the pressure becomes too much, Melissa turns to strict dieting to regain control. Young women will find real-life situations and relatable characters as they read of Melissa's struggle with anorexia.

The Big Picture
Jenny B. Jones
ISBN-13: 978-1-60006-208-7
ISBN-10: 1-60006-208-3

The third book in THE KATIE PARKER PRODUCTION series. Bobbie Ann Parker, released from prison, wants to start a new life with her daughter—in a new town. Katie is forced to walk away from In Between, leaving the family she loves, an endangered town drive-in, and a boyfriend who suddenly can't take his eyes off his ex.

My Beautiful Disaster
Michelle Buckman
ISBN-13: 978-1-60006-083-0
ISBN-10: 1-60006-083-8

Hanging out with Heather and Tammy, the most popular girls in school, has changed Dixie's life. Every weekend is filled with shopping trips, pizza, and parties. But no escapade compares to the night the three of them sneak out to see a hot new band.

To order copies, visit your local Christian bookstore, call NavPress at
1-800-366-7788, or log on to www.navpress.com.
To locate a Christian bookstore near you, call 1-800-991-7747.